TERRIAN JOURNALS'

POLITICAL
SCIENCE
FICTION

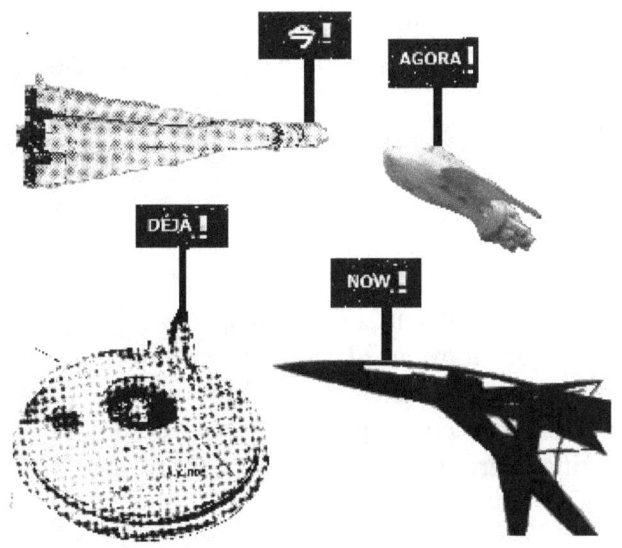

by Donald Murray Anderson

(author of the Terrian Journals series)

Terrian Journals' Political Science Fiction
A Mythbreaker Book
First Edition updated 2026
© Copyright 2021 by Donald Murray Anderson

ISBN 978-1-989593-24-0

For information address: mythbreaker@mail.com

Preface

Political science fiction is a well-established genre which includes classics such as <u>Looking Backward</u>, <u>The Time Machine</u>, <u>1984</u>, and <u>The Martian Chronicles</u>, along with motion pictures including "Things To Come" (based on a book by the same author as <u>The Time Machine)</u>, "The Day The Earth Stood Still", "Logan's Run", "Black Panther", "The Net", "Enemy of The State", "Déjà Vu", and "Star Trek: Insurrection".

Even "Star Wars" makes a political statement by pitting opposing monarchical dictatorships against each other.

Political science fiction is distinct from pure science fiction which marvels at and dwells upon innovative technologies, alien encounters, and the exploration of the far reaches of outer space in their own right.

Political science fiction looks at the implications of all of the above science fiction, with particular attention to the socio-political implications and potential outcomes.

Introduction

The very existence of this book of fiction surprises me because I only write non-fiction in the <u>Terrian Journals</u> series.

By its very nature, <u>Terrian Journals,</u> which is a diary of thoughts in adventure, can only be non-fiction.

However, with two exceptions, "Feast and Famine" and "One of Six", <u>Terrian Journals' Political Science Fiction</u> is inspired by actual events in the sense of the real life experiences that inspire me to write the fiction.

Yet the two exceptions are truly <u>Terrian Journals</u> thoughts in adventure.

In that sense, "Feast and Famine" and "One of Six" are not entirely exceptional in my writing. They remain, however, the only short stories converted from screenplays in this book.

I remain, above all, a writer of non-fiction, not fiction, for reasons that I explain while I'm delayed waiting for budget airline ticket offices to reopen after a public holiday in Xiang Giang.

I use the undesired inactivity to finish reading a fiction book that I buy in Australia a few days earlier. I rarely buy or read fiction.

This atypical reading prompts me to write some paragraphs differentiating my writing from fiction and explaining my preference for non-fiction.

I recognize that a diary of thoughts in adventures as they happen recounts stories that are often, as the expression says, stranger than fiction.

Why I don't usually write fiction:

Days in Capricornia

Staying here in Xiang Giang because of circumstances instead of free choice, being obliged to be inactive and inert instead of exploring new territory or enjoying former discoveries, annoys me.

But there is a positive side. The days are 10°C, much cooler than other recent places. This enables me to more gradually adjust to the cooler days ahead as I go farther north.

It's barely the start of spring there now.

I can also profit from the inactivity to finish the Australian book I begin reading a couple of days ago in Darwin. It's called Capricornia.

It's a fascinating book set about 52 years before I read it.

Capricornia presents the relationships and problems which develop between the Aboriginal and European Australians during that era.

Reading this book just after visiting the middle of Australia makes me wonder if much changes there in 52 years. I see continuing racism in Australia and not only against Aborigines.

The book is so interesting and well-written that I read 100 of the 500 pages during my flights here. By the time I can get out of Xiang Giang I can finish the whole book.

My hunger for reading material is evident in the way that I devour Capricornia.

I prefer non-fiction 1,000 times, but the value of reading this novel is that it quickly demystifies novel writing for me. It's a kind of pattern writing much like an essay.

Begin a story, make characters disappear then reappear to twig and revive the reader's interest.

So much of the anglo writing that I'm exposed to since childhood seems to be just trying to multiply tragic outcomes and to thus brutalize the reader in a similar way to violence in negative movies.

It's debilitating conditioning.

So much the better that I prefer non-fiction, even if everyone in every true story eventually dies.

I realize that fiction is a useful way of portraying the mood of times, places, and events.

At the same time, fictional characters can be used like puppets to put forward points of view that challenge ideas in vogue, societies in place, and regimes in power.

Thus the author can comment on his/her society while somewhat buffering and protecting her/himself from irrational reactions by putting his comments into the mouths of non-existent people.

If necessary, they can take the blame for the author's most critical and severe criticisms and thoughts.

My preference for non-fiction is based on the fact that it's required to be an accurate description of reality, not a modified, embroidered, dramatized, or elaborate portrayal.

Non-fiction contains factual information which enables the reader to cross-check, compare, and quote the writer as a reference.

The reader can acquire knowledge of accurate details, draw his/her own conclusions, and seek other interpretations.

Non-fiction prohibits the author from single-handedly constructing every personality and everything else.

S/he has to base his/her writing on authenticated information describing the details of actual, living people and their true life experiences.

Non-fiction writing cannot diverge from this factual information. The non-fiction writer isn't permitted to make up people or events.

Such invention discredits the author, his/her work and conclusions.

A non-fiction writer has to be able to substantiate all statements of fact and build all points of view expressed from a body of facts which are widely available.

The words of a person speaking in non-fiction cannot be made up.

At its best, non-fiction can be an unedited excerpt from reality.

Reality, non-fiction writing appeals to me because reality is a setting in which there is at least some possibility to change outcomes based on knowledge.

In fiction there's no such option.

Good non-fiction illustrates how actual living people, not fabricated characters, face certain real decisions and take certain concrete actions or fail to act, which leads to outcomes which are predictable and unpredictable.

Like the reality that it describes, non-fiction isn't set and fixed at the outset. Non-fiction tells what happens to real people because of their choices.

Being factual makes non-fiction all the more interesting, often amazing, and always exemplary.

In contrast, the information in fiction can be faulty and false. Fiction writing can thus undermine the writer's credibility. It will definitely misinform the readers.

This is a common and often justified criticism of U.S. movie plots which are "based on actual events" but stray into fictionalized characters, scenes, and events.

Examples include "Cleopatra", staring Elizabeth Taylor and the screenplay rewrite of William Lishman's true story, Father Goose.

The viewpoint in fiction is also liable to be completely subjective without any foundation in fact beyond the writer's combining and rewriting of unrelated personal incidents and people met, along with personal opinions and prejudices.

A reader may not have the means, resources, or motivation to attempt to check the source of an author's information or the basis of his/her views.

There are no "primary sources" for fiction beyond the author's mind.

The characters never live. The characters never take part in real events. Their experiences never happen. They never make real choices.

The characters leave no diaries, letters, or friends and families to help the reader learn more about the characters or to come up with a perspective of the characters which is different from the author's description.

By the very nature of fiction writing, the author is the only witness to the non-existent life of the non-existent characters.

The author alone makes all of the choices during the characters' entire existence.

The duration of that existence is confined to the number pages about her/his "life" in the writing created by the author and the length restrictions stipulated by the editors and publishers.

Characters like Lucy Maude Montgomery's Anne are rare exceptions. Despite Montgomery's desire to put an end to Anne books, Anne lives almost as long as Montgomery.

The lifespan of Montgomery's Anne books appears to be indefinite.

The Japanese school system immortalizes Anne by adopting her first story as a text book in translation.

Long after Montgomery's death, screenplay writers capitalizes on Anne's enduring popularity by turning her into an eternally young time traveller who has an adventure during the 1914-1918 war.

If Montgomery's Anne were portrayed accurately, she would be ancient or dead, not a young woman during that war.

Fiction stories are also a closed system. A reader's presence is sought for the sole purpose of finding out what a single writer has to relate about what s/he invents.

The author provides no references or sources of opposing or even supporting views. There's no question and answer session at the end for readers.

A reader may agree or disagree with the author's perspective, but there's no response card attached to the final page. After reading the last page, the book is finished.

The reader is dealing with no more than a composite view of some of the author's personal experiences and interpretations.

The reader might also be exposed to accurate but uncited research findings described indirectly through made-up people, places, and/or stories which never exist.

Only the author knows.

Fiction can be a pure invention wherein actors and sets stand in for real people and places.

When facts are slipped in here and there, how can the reader differentiate between them and fantasy?

No matter how elaborate or detailed fiction becomes, it's not a strictly factual recounting of true tales about persons who live.

Nor is fiction under any obligation to accurately relate situations or historic settings which actually occur and exist.

No matter how lifelike the characters may seem, no matter how credible and entrancing the stories become, no matter how well characters and settings reflect actual times, real events and places, they're just the writer's re-fabrication and rearrangement of realities.

Fictitious stories aren't realities themselves.

Fiction is based entirely upon a complete, premeditated, careful, deliberate, and sometimes clever reconstruction of excerpts from reality by the writer.

The writing which results can reflect reality, but it is not reality.

The better the fiction writing and the better the invention, the more a reader will like it and the more a reader may perceive fiction as reality.

Fiction can take readers' minds far away from the workings of reality. No matter what the writer's intentions, the credibility of his/her writing can become its key ingredient.

Credibility can make the reader lose touch with reality even when s/he's not reading. This has implications because a work of credible fiction includes a world outlook.

Regardless of the specific author, story, and messages, the world outlook to which I refer is a constant. It's the same and common to all fiction.

The fiction world outlook is the predetermined storyline.

It's decided by the author alone. S/he's not simply recording chance occurrences as they happen. S/he controls chance.

No one else has a choice of outcomes.

The reader of any work of fiction is thus given an intricately planned and well thought-out illusion from the very outset.

S/he is being persuaded that s/he is entering a complete, fixed, artificial environment which supports life.

The writer's careful planning and construction of his/her writing convinces the reader that the environment really exists.

Of course it does not exist. It also cannot support life.

The fictitious world is a place where all is predestined. No matter what people do, their efforts to change the storyline will be futile.

For this fictitious world to absorb the readers' mind, s/he needs to have the perception that the persons and events in the environment are credible.

Quality fiction writing makes this happen.

Once the reader accepts the characters and events, s/he begins to perceive the artificial as real or natural.

The reader is becoming a passive, accepting creature in the fiction writer's preserve.

In the fiction writer's preserve, the writer is an invisible, omnipresent, omnipotent deity. S/he makes unilateral decisions before the reader arrives.

Her/his writing only describes what s/he dictates and makes up. His/her writing is based exclusively on her/his decisions about character behaviour and choices.

The beginning and events don't constitute a factual recounting of some true event as it naturally begins and unfolds.

The fiction writer decides to add and omit, to eliminate choice, and to fix all outcomes before the writing is put into final print.

The fiction writer's preserve is prearranged, based entirely on the extrapolation of just his/her experiences and knowledge into his/her thoughts and outlook.

The resulting story is planned to lead to only one possible conclusion, regardless of the reader's identity. The reader has no choice, option, or alternative.

Only the writer's intended messages are available.

The overriding impression left by reading any credible fiction is thus no more than a belief in the author deity and the absorption of his/her message.

A story invented and dictated by only one person can thus create the impression, by the nature of the type of writing itself, that life is predetermined and full of preordained truths, just like fiction.

Life is then perceived as an unalterable rigidity of characters, outcomes, beliefs, and conclusions. It's a form of churchism or ideologism.

Readers, like characters, may come to believe and resign themselves to outcomes in life over which they have no choice and in which they have no say.

A work of fiction is much like a work of architecture created by experts, in almost total isolation from the people who are the ultimate users and captives of the housing or workplace which the experts alone create.

The only role of the user in this type of structure is to just accept that which has been created and imposed by someone else.

Unlike reality, s/he can do nothing to change the story.

A reader of fiction can only agree or disagree with the viewpoint, like or dislike the givens of the story and storytelling. S/he cannot change them.

S/he is forced to conclude that although s/he may not like aspects of the story, s/he cannot do anything about it.

A serious problem can arise if, by entering this fictional domain too often or too completely, a reader is persuaded that not only fiction is lifelike, but that life is also fiction-like.

In life beyond fiction too, s/he may thus come to perceive him/herself as no more than an observer, unable to change, unable to influence outcomes.

"C'est la vie!" s/he mournfully declares. Fiction writing and reading can thus be far more a lesson in non-participatory democratic behaviour.

Fiction writing can be a lesson in passivity derived from an imposed sense of impotence or frustration.

Or it may be a lesson in believing that "everything will be all right in the end", so no participation is necessary.

Thus it's essential not to lose sight of reality while reading fiction. A reader must recognize both for what they are, distinct and separate realms.

In reality, character behaviour and choices depend on a variety of individuals and groups and what actually happens, i.e. unpredictable events. Coincidence intervenes.

The way that a person behaves depends upon her/his interactions with other, different, real, living and breathing persons who behave in often unexpected, surprising, and unforeseeable ways when they find themselves in circumstances that they do partially control, or don't control largely because of a lack of volition.

Reality is non-fiction and vice versa.

I find reality and the non-fiction that it creates so enthralling. I find it has much variety, many options, choices, and possible outcomes.

That's why I prefer non-fiction to fiction.

[And yet along the way I write 16 fictional stories, based on actual thoughts in adventure, and they become the content of Terrian Journals' Political Science Fiction.]

Note:

Some of the stories in this volume are reproduced and edited directly from the pages of core books in the Terrian Journals series.

Others, such as "Remains" and "In A Perfect World" are stories written for Terrian Journals' Political Science Fiction as the expansion of ideas for writing described in passing in the core books of Terrian Journals.

The Stories

Alien Flew

Unsurveyed Planet: 4972616557311009

Following the discovery of an obscure new planet in a far away galaxy, an investigatory probe is sent to catalogue the planetary environment and any life forms within it.

This is the report of the investigatory probe:

Both airborne and surface life forms are prevalent. They are generally smaller than 60 centimetres in diameter, with some much larger exceptions.

Both forms share a symbiotic relationship.

They survive and flourish everywhere on the planetary surface by applying their natural intelligence without artificial life support of any type.

The entire planetary environment and all the other forms of life on the planet are dependent on the prevalent lifeforms.

There are larger forms of life on the planet, including those living in the planet's liquid environment, but they are smaller in number than the dominant life forms and will accordingly be explained later.

We recommend attempting to communicate with the dominant air and surface life forms.

There are very strong indications that these lifeforms are the most intelligent forms of life on this planet.

They have developed the most adaptable and environmentally appropriate, complex, intricate, and enduring behaviours, predating all the less abundant forms of life on the planet.

They have also developed a means of intelligent commu-nication which challenges the most advanced decoding comprehension skills known to our world.

Their encoding and decoding requires the application of more in-tellect than any of the other life forms on the planet.

None of those life forms appear to have the intelligence required to communicate with the planet's dominant forms of life.

There is only one apparent predatory species threatening and en-dangering the dominant life forms and the environmental system that they ensure.

The predator is a larger land species, sometimes measuring two metres or more in length, but more commonly not exceeding 1.67 metres.

Width varies, although most specimens of the predator fall within the range of no more than 90 centimetres in dia-meter, but a large number far exceed that dimension.

Lacking advanced intelligence, the predator's sole survival skill appears to be to overtly and indirectly attack and kill the planet's predominant lifeforms and all of the others.

The predator is most accurately described as essentially a parasite rather than a self-sufficient and independent life form.

The predator's lack of survival skills and destructive behaviour are manifestations of lower intelligence and sheer clumsiness.

The predator is an awkward form of life which appears to have no purpose or intent beyond preying upon more intelligent life forms.

Further planetary studies are needed to assess the extent of the predator's threat to intelligent planetary life.

But some preliminary intervention seems necessary to mitigate the impact of the predator's destructive behaviour and negative impact on the dominant life forms and their life support systems.

The predator's menacing behaviour toward intelligent life on the planet needs to be checked...

Nine hundred millennia later -

True News reports alien presence detection:

"Our final story tonight already has our newsroom laughing.

"A hermit showed up in a remote third world village today claiming that he has an ear infection caused by aliens.

"The local medicine man is trying to assure him that it's all in his dirty mind. Apparently the hermit washes very infrequently and forgets to clean out his ears.

"GET YOURSELF SOME COTTON SWABS!

"And that's it for us. Stay tuned for tonight's three hour specials here on Reality TV. Until next time, GET REAL!"

A remote "third" world village:

"I know what you're thinking, doc. I'm staying to myself too much, not looking after myself. But this ear infection is different." Zek the hermit says.

Sighing, Dr. Yot says, "Well this infection does look bad, I'll grant you that. But aliens! Have you been eating too many contaminated grubs and mushrooms?"

"If I were that stupid, I'd be a long time dead."

"But why blame 'aliens' Zek? I may be a country doctor, but that's not a cause of ear infection that's in my medical journals."

"I already told you about that Dr. Yot. Something from outer space zapped me in the ear while I was getting ready to sleep. Up until then, I was feeling a hundred percent."

"Well Zek, I'm going to give you some pills and cream. That should drive out the aliens in your head, I mean your ear."

. . . . .

Three days later, the police arrive at the doctor's door. Officer Glan is shaking a pill bottle in front of the Dr. Yot's eyes.

"Are these yours doc?"

"Why yes. How did you get them Glan? Did that fool Zek throw them away!? I'll have to get after him."

Glan looks down and says, "He's right outside doc. But you're too late. Zek's dead."

"Wh..what!" the doctor stammers. "That can't be. All he had was a bad ear infection."

"Can you do an autopsy doc, to determine the cause of death?"

"It's been a while, but sure. Bring him in."

After carefully examining Zek's body, Dr. Yot looks gravely at Officer Glan.

"Well Glan, I can't find any particular cause of death. The ear infection is worse than it was, but that can't be what killed Zek.

"I'll have to send these tissue samples to a lab in the big city. It might take months to get back the results that I need to determine the exact cause of death.

"Now it looks as if Zek just dropped dead of natural causes. He had a hard life, living out there all by himself."

. . . . .

A year later Dr. Yot gets the lab report. He calls at Officer Glan's office.

"Just as I thought, natural causes. Zek's body just gave out. There's nothing definitive on the ear infection, but he lived in a very dirty environment, so the infection could be caused by a lot of things."

"Not aliens Dr. Yot?" Glan smiles. "Zek was quite a character." They both laugh.

That same year, many people die after suffering from ear infections in remote places that know nothing about Zek, Yot, or Glan.

Reports are scattered and no connection between the infections and death are found.

There are always people dying for various reasons in places that are invisible to the rest of the world.

During the following decades the number of people reporting ear infections and subsequently dying increases a hundred fold, but almost unperceived at the WHO.

The rising number of ear infections is officially recorded. This leads to increased funding of research in that field and survivors of the ear infection victims form support groups.

Eventually, researchers find commonalities in the ear infections and determine that the probable cause is some form of virus. There is no apparent cure.

Since the largest number of ear infection patients live in the "third" world, it is difficult to obtain funding for developing improved treatment and medications to help combat the virus. Pharmaceutical companies see no profit in it.

It's like malaria. It's not contagious. It doesn't cross the ocean. So it's not a "first" world problem.

As the decades pass and ear infections increase unchecked, there is an apparently coincidental significant decline in the population of the "third" world.

"First" world leaders conclude that the world population is naturally levelling off and note that the number of people living in poverty and suffering from malnutrition are also declining.

This news is celebrated and attributed to medical advances, an increase in food supplies, and generous foreign aid.

Progress Report Update:

Re: Unsurveyed Planet: 4972616557311009

The ongoing intervention project is progressing as planned. The population of the predator threatening the dominant life forms on this planet is declining.

Our invasion of the aural cavities of the largest part of the predator population continues unperceived and unhindered by the predator.

The low intelligence of the predator has not been under-estimated. According to current estimates, 200 million predators have already been eliminated.

The rate of elimination is increasing exponentially from 100 million during the first year to an additional 100 million within the following six months.

Our successful termination of about 1% of the predator population through our previous major invasion, a century earlier, may
now be exceeded.

Continuing the corporeal invasions of the past three thousand
years is projected to eventually result in eradicating the predator
as a planet-wide threat.

The survival and fruition of the most prevalent and intelligent life
forms on the planet, avian and entomological, is becoming more
certain as the predators disappear.

Remains

The news is catching us all by surprise. We know it's going to happen, but we're not expecting it to be now.

It's a kind of religion that we all believe without any real, true, solid evidence. Yet there it is, undeniable proof positive.

We've found it at last! Well, at least the scientists have found it.

We now know for sure that there is other intelligent life somewhere far away in the universe.

They've found an actual, real life ETs, extraterrestrials, orbiting around a planet in a distant solar system.

One of the space probes we sent out 40 years ago picked up the signal ten years ago.

We sent a more advanced, much faster probe ten years ago to go directly to the planet.

That probe is sending back the data analyzing the life in orbit around the planet.

A PL, planet lander, sent more recently is now arriving on the planet surface, exploring various sites and sending back more information about the orbiting life's home planet.

Unfortunately, the aliens orbiting the planet are all dead, having run out of comestibles, including the mostly nitro-gen/oxygen gas atmosphere sustaining them.

Much the same can be said for the planetary surface.

The positive result of this total absence of atmosphere in the spacecraft is the perfect mummification of the aliens.

So we have perfect specimens of the planet's only apparent space-faring form of life.

Their relatively tiny spacecraft is barely large enough to house the aliens aboard.

Our PL is finding the partial skeletal remains of numerous other members of the same species strewn across the planetary surface, along with a multitude of other species.

Apparently they are all extinct.

The only forms of life now inhabiting the planet are avian and entomological, in apparently perfect symbiotic relationships.

According to data transmitted to date, the orbiting aliens also had a symbiotic relationship with another form of life.

The other form seems to have been a species serving the main species.

The serving species had limb appendages enabling it to perform many useful tasks for the main species and was apparently trained to operate certain technologies and to develop other, pad-like devices enabling the main species to reduce the need for using the serving species.

The language or languages of the aliens has yet to be deciphered.

Although the orbiting spacecraft provide some language clues, comparison is difficult because each craft found to date has different types of symbols embossed on it.

One craft has what appears to be a tricolour, primitive bar code, comprised of horizontal lines and a corner with circles having pointed edges.

Another spacecraft, one slightly older, has a more intricate pattern.

It's comprised of a somewhat rectangular object and a diagonal open circle.

A long diagonal line originating at the lower edge of the rectangular object crosses the open circle, making the two objects overlap.

There are other different symbols on each spacecraft, per-haps a form of primitive language characters.

The older craft has three very simple, identical half-circle characters opening to the right, followed by a half circle opening to the right with a line closing it and stretching below it.

The more recent craft has three distinct characters.

They are an upward opening elongated circle, two linked but opposite open circles, and an open triangle shape, point up, with a line crossing it at the centre.

A much newer spacecraft has another set of markings which are far more intricate than the other two types, indicating a more intellectually evolved form of the space-faring aliens.

The markings are:

1) a long horizontal box with a vertical line crossing it from top to bottom at the centre and extending beyond both the top and bottom of the box; and,

2) a square of equal size to the entire first marking.

The square contains three horizontal lines with spaces on each side. The top and bottom lines are of equal length and longer than the line in the middle.

One vertical line joins the three horizontal lines but it does not extend beyond the top and bottom.

There is also a very small, left up and right down diagonal line suspended on the right side between the middle and bottom horizontal lines inside the box.

The marking looks like this: 中国.

Life on Mars

Exobiologists are now receiving signals from the Mars RCRV launched nearly a year ago and presumed lost.

RCRV has successfully landed on the planetary surface at a landing site in a near polar region which looks very promising. Scientists call it "Tupicia".

It is currently summer there and temperature readings are in the cool to moderate range.

The world's most advanced bio-motion scanners are fully functional.

RCRV's life sensing capabilities are far beyond the rolling and shovelling chemistry sets of the old Martian rovers with their presbyopic cameras.

Rovers were restricted to looking for evidence of micro-organisms and the conditions suitable for supporting them on Mars.

Rovers cameras were bind to larger forms of Martian life that might move right in front of the rover cameras.

RCRV can detect the presence and movement of very large and complex organisms displaying characteristics similar to Earth species.

Unfortunately, the command mechanism of the RCRV cameras appears to have been damaged by an unexpectedly hard landing.

But scientists are attempting to bring them on line.

Despite the camera problem, an advanced search for life on Mars is finally underway.

Tupicia, Near Polar Region

RCRV lands on the planet with a burst of crystals flying into the upper air, spreading a thick layer of icy debris over the lander and all that surrounds the landing site.

Startled and bewildered, the life forms of the planet scatter in all directions, evading the probing sensors of the invading spacecraft.

Nak can't move. She's buried in the artificial blizzard-like storm before she can scramble away from it. This also prevents RCRV from detecting her.

Her small band of companions soon come to her rescue and dig her out. A beam of light scans them from the RCRV as they pull Nak out.

Everyone runs to avoid the beam, fearing it may be a concentrated solar flare that could burn them.

The atmosphere has become much thinner since the environment began to change.

Safely out of range, Nak and her companions look carefully and follow the light beam to its source.

It's not coming from off the planet. It's originating in an ice crater now apparent in the near distance.

Crawling toward the crater, Nak evades the light beam and peaks over the side of the crater. An orb about 1.5 metres in diameter is emitting the beam.

Nak's companions creep after her and join her in their expressions of astonishment. Whatever can that thing be?

Curiosity and courage overcome surprise and any sense of fear.

The "Tupician" group experiments by throwing snowballs toward the light beam.

It follows the crystal decoys, enabling the group to approach the orb and tap on its shiny covering.

This catches the light beam's attention and it swings a broad beam around the entire circumference of the orb.

Nak and her companions jump back, but too late to avoid the now broadening beam. They are unscathed. It is as harmless to them as a vehicle headlight.

Emboldened by the apparent harmlessness of the invading orb, Nak approaches again and begins rubbing the debris from landing that's covering the top of the orb.

She finds strange markings on the orb.

<u>RCRV HQ</u>

Months later, exobiologists at RCRV mission control receive the signal relayed to them by a communication satellite orbiting Mars.

They scientists cheer as they announce to the world that RCRV has found evidence of a large, but still unidentified form of life on Mars.

"The founding people of the space age are today celebrating another historic feat.

"We have discovered a new world of life!" the RCRV project director proudly declares before a room packed with news cameras and reporters.

"Within the next twelve months we will attempt first contact with the Martians.

"The launch of a new Martian probe is imminent. This one will contain only a 360 degree array of cameras and microphones.

"There will also be a recording broadcasting only one word, 'Peace' in each of our 6,000 human languages."

. . . . .

Meanwhile, in Tupicia, long before this news conference, Nak is copying the orb's strange markings onto a large piece of bone.

After the hunting season and the long months of winter that follow, Nak will make the long trek to a large population centre farther south so that the elders can explain the markings to her.

Only they will be able to tell her the meaning of "РОССИЯ" when she arrives in Iqaluit.

Mediums rare

The anonymity of computer contact, along with the use of avatars and facial modifying software put Internet system users in touch with entities they cannot truly see or encounter in daily life.

Many people use the computer medium to become official friends with the strange entities that they are unlikely to ever meet.

Consequently, scepticism and criticism of mediums takes a new and novel turn.

People who spend all their lives contacting modified and invisible "friends" via the computer medium find this contact so routine and normal that they forget that the entities are based on actual people.

Medium users lose the ability to distinguish between real and artificial intelligence.

This status quo carries on without question or notice until one day someone tells a story about having the ability to communicate without using computers or Internet servers.

This person sends out a message stating that she is communicating directly with other people, in person.

It's a wireless communications system that she calls "in the flesh".

She claims that she can actually see the natural corporeal forms and faces of people in front of her naked eyes, without using a viewscreen.

She's hearing things too. She claims that she can hear them without a headset or loud speakers.

She declares that their vocal cords are creating a sound which she calls "speech".

She actually believes that she can smell and touch them too.

Anonymous on-line comments abound, discrediting the obvious hoaxter:

"She must be either a delusional raving lunatic or a shameless fraud, faker, and liar."

"Only very gullible people would ever believe such non-sense."

"Is she asking people to pay her money to communicate directly without a screen?"

"How can anyone communicate with live spirits using only eyes, ears, nose, and tactile senses?"

"What an extraordinary claim to make! Science can easily disprove it and expose the charlatans professing to have the power to connect using only human senses."

In A Perfect World

Nobody knows when it happened or why. In fact, nobody knows what happened.

My 103 year old grandma tells many stories during the 33 years I know her, but she never mentions it. She must know. She remembers everything else about her life.

Thinking about it is very strange. I don't know why I'm doing it. I just can't help being curious about everything.

Everybody says, "Just enjoy our perfect world. It doesn't matter why it's perfect. You don't have to talk about it. You don't even have to think about it. It's perfect. Leave it at that."

Taking a walk always gets me thinking, but this particular day I see something that surprises me. It always happens. That's one of the wonders of living in the perfect world.

But today really is different. I'm somewhere on the edge of the world, going along the perimeter of nowhere.

Nowhere is what doesn't matter. It's outside the perfect world, so nobody is interested in it. I'm not either, but I can't stop thinking about it, especially today.

When I pass by a water pond I catch a glimpse of something in the water, something unusually strange and alien. It's the first time I see anything like it.

It seems to be a different life form. That's not so unusual. In the perfect world different forms of life often appear and disappear.

But this one is different. It's some sort of mimic, like the robotoids in the parks. But they stay on dry land. And what I see is not a robotoid.

Robotoids replicate in exact detail the person they're mimicking. It's like looking at your twin when you don't have one.

Actually, I don't know what a twin is. I never see one, I mean two. So maybe they are a myth. Why would two people ever look alike anyway? It's not necessary.

There I go again, confounding even myself with my curiosity.

The life form that I see in the water does not change to mimic me, yet it does. But in action alone, not in appearance.

Without changing form, the water mimic does exactly what I do and exactly when I do it.

But by not mimicking my appearance, the mimic is such a novelty. It's perfectly amazing.

It's easy to understand why the water mimic puzzles me. The robotoids never behaves this way. That's their charm.

They are lots of fun. They make everyone laugh every day. That's part of what the perfect world is all about.

The robotoid is so perfect at mimicking that it's perfectly hilarious.

But again, somehow the water mimic replicates only my motions, not myself. It looks completely different from me. It's so perfectly strange.

Like a robotoid, the water mimic copies everything that I do instantly in complete details. But unlike the robotoid, the water mimic does not replicate my face and body.

It's perplexing. It's almost as if the water mimic were not perfect. But that's impossible. Everything is always perfect in a perfect world.

Well, maybe not everything. Otherwise we would all remember when it starts, and why.

I have to go back for another look. Maybe I need a sensory tune-eup.

·····

The next time I go to the perimeter of nowhere again, I find the water mimic waiting for me, as if it knows when to expect me. That's not unusual in a perfect world.

I try the line that some people use for amusing themselves with the robotoids. I look straight into the water mimic's strange face and eyes and say, "I am you."

The water mimic has no voice! Unbelievable!

Its strange lips can only duplicate the motion of my own lips at exactly the same moment and in exactly the same way as I move them.

Perfectly wonderful!

I'm so amused that I fall down laughing, slipping my toes into the cool water as I hit the ground.

This causes a delightfully unexpected surprise. When the water ripples at the touch of my wiggling toes, the water mimic ripples with it. How perfectly extraordinary!

Robotoid mimics don't ripple in the wind. The water mimic must be an innovation. Its strange features become stranger as they ripple with the water.

I burst into laughter again.

Is the perfect world becoming more perfect by introducing this mute and non-identical mimic?

I will start coming here regularly.

On a day of perfect weather, I decide to go for a dip and play with the mute water mimic in its own medium.

Of course every day has perfect weather. It's perfectly sunny, rainy, snowy, cloudy, stormy, etc.

It's just like our routine daily greetings: "How are you? I'm perfect. And you? I'm perfect. Thank you."

When I dive into the pond I expect to see the water mimic jumping into the air. Maybe it will ripple in the air. How perfectly marvellous!

My perfect astonishment surprises me when, at the moment I submerse myself in liquid, the water mimic completely disappears.

Where could it possibly go?

I swim deeper but find no trace of it. I look to the water surface above but see only light refracting overhead. It's perfectly whetting my curiosity.

Robotoids can't do this magic trick. They're always there, no matter what we do.

Returning to the air I find no water mimic waiting for me, neither floating nor rippling. Perfectly mysterious.

Then I spot its head. It's not in front of me or behind me. It's right under my head. It copies my surprised facial expression perfectly.

All I can see is the water mimic's head. Then, as I leave the water, the entire mimic reappears. This mimic is perfectly amazing.

It's at this moment that I realize I'm in unfamiliar surroundings. In my underwater search for the mimic I swim far from the shore where I dive in.

Before I can look across the horizons to locate my starting point, I hear a distance voice approaching and calling out to me.

"What are you doing here?"

I reply with the customary, "Having a perfectly good time."

The voice's response is gruff and most unusual, "Not on this shore you're not. You're in Row. How did you get here?"

I don't know what to say. What's Row? I can only reply with the normal "That's perfectly obvious."

Retorting, "There you go again! What's all this "perfect" about? Are you a vocabulary deficient?"

I have no idea. I wonder what "deficient" means. Before I can ask, the voice continues:

"You look normal."

"Normal?" I say, wondering what this word means too. "I'm perfect."

Laughing, the voice replies, "Have it your way. I know a good word usage consultant if you want to expand..."

"I don't expand." That's a word I do know. "I'm perfect."

"Yah, right." the voice says, with a more subdued laugh.

Finally, the body connected to the voice appears from behind the bushes beside the pond, lowering her voice volume as she gets closer.

She looks strange, like the water mimic. I don't know how to describe her. The word "perfect" somehow seems bizarrely unsuitable and inappropriate. How can that be?

Is she a robotoid in the process of transforming from someone else? I've never seen a person looking anything like her.

"What happened to your eye?" she says.

"Nothing. My eyes are perfect."

"Yah... well, let's go to the clinic and get an expert to take a look at you."

She leads me through the bush onto a strange road to a strange building. She puts her hand on a metal bulb on part of the wall and pulls until that part swings out toward us.

We walk through and she pushes the wall part back into place.

It's like a non-sliding door that doesn't automatically open and close when approached. How strange. Not perfect?

The next sight is equally strange. There's someone inside the building who also looks like the water mimic, instead of a perfect person. Am I in an experimental robotoid zone?

I call the ones I'm seeing "strangers". It seems appropriate and suits their appearances. Yes, appearances. They aren't either similar or identical like the robotoids.

The shore stranger isn't transforming or performing tricks. The building stranger is looking straight into my perfect eyes.

"Having vision problems?" she asks. "My vision is perfect." I say. Shore stranger interjects, "Don't pay her any mind. She's vocabulary deficient."

"I'm perfect." I reply nonchalantly. Shore stranger giggles.

"Well your 'perfect' eyes seem to need adjusting." building stranger says. "You have some sort of implants and they appear to be malfunctioning."

I'm about to say, "They're perfect." but I hesitate. A slight adjustment may be required since I am seeing strangers instead of my perfect world peers.

A small tune-up will enable me to see the strangers as they truly are, instead of their strange appearances.

In a moment the adjustment is made, but when I open my eyes again I'm still seeing strangers. I'm feeling somewhat disconcerted, perfectly of course.

"I think it will take me a while to adapt to the adjustment. Thank you for your perfect help." I say.

Shore stranger snickers as she touches the bulb on the wall, repeating the wall opening and closing again. We are outdoors once more.

"I'll take you into town to see if we can get you some more vocabulary." she says. "That will be perfect." I reply.

"Enough! Give it a rest."

"What's it?" I wonder out loud.

"You're perfectly hilarious." she says, laughing at her own joke. I respond with a perfect laugh.

This is the most remarkable day of my life. The "town" is hardly that. It's a collection of small buildings much like the one where I get my vision adjustment.

It's an incomprehensible town with buildings that lack perfection. There, I've thought it. They aren't perfect.

That's only the beginning of my day. Then I see the town inhabitants. More strangers. And they aren't perfect strangers. They all lack perfection.

Using customary language to describe all that I see, I would say "perfectly awful". The words never leave my lips but they hover in my mind.

For the rest of the day I can't say the word "perfect", much to the surprise of the shore stranger.

Instead of my daily sightings of perfect people, perfect places, and perfect lives in a perfect world, I'm having visions of quite extraordinary people and things.

There are no perfect faces, bodies, or buildings. If I report this problem to the authorities in my perfect world, they might think I've gone perfectly mad.

Shore stranger can apparently sense my distress and tells me I should go home and rest until I can absorb everything that I'm seeing. She's perfectly right.

She takes me back to the pond and points toward the shore where I jumped in. All I have to do is swim straight toward a large tree over there.

I bid shore stranger farewell and dive into the pond, saying, "Have a perfect day!" She says, "I'll try." followed by a set of parting words entirely new to me.

"Please come again. Don't be a stranger."

I'm in the water. So all I can do is think, "Of course not. I'm perfect."

I rise straight out of the water when I reach the large tree, not pausing to look back to see the water mimic who must be right behind me as I emerge from the liquid.

I'm in familiar territory now and find my way back to the centre of the perfect world very easily.

I feel perfectly fine and ready to carry on with a perfect day.
But there's something wrong. The perfect world is suddenly different. People and places are no longer perfect.

I'm seeing flaws.

There are all variety of faces and bodies with what can only be described as imperfections. I seem to be inventing a word.

It's disconcerting. To reassure myself, I look into my self-reflecting screen. What I see makes me grimace as never before.

My grimace is the only thing reflecting back at me that I can call a perfect image. The face I see on screen is not my perfect self at all. It is the water mimic in the pond.

I rush back to the pond and confirm that the mimic and my screen self appear to be exactly the same. The water mimic looks as puzzled as I am.

Without changing into swim clothes I plunge back into the pond and stroke heavily until I finally reach the shore where I meet the shore stranger.

She's already there waiting for me, as if expecting my return.

"Don't worry." she says. "Your vision certainly is perfect now. The implants really were defective. That's why you could see your actual self reflecting in the pond."

"Our doctor simply removed the implants instead of repairing them. So now you can see everything as it truly is, instead of its perfect image."

"You are now in ROW, the real outside world. In fact, it's the real world, not outside or inside out.

"Free of your unreal virtual reality, you can now try to understand the real world perfectly well and help to improve it toward real perfection.

You have left the isolating illusions of perfect appearances behind you."

What a perfectly novel idea!

Wheelies

People with wheels, the wheelies, go everywhere on wheels. Wheels are a necessity. How can anyone live without them?

Yes, the less fortunate have none. So the wheelies help them by donating surplus, outmoded parts that are no longer needed, parts long abandoned by wheelies.

These parts are widely known as extrems or spare limbs. With a little conditioning they can be used by the less fortunate.

The extrems are appended to mobilize the less fortunate who have no mobility.

Donating extrems is becoming quite a popular craze among the wheelies.

It's relatively painless for the wheelies.

They possess a conditioned reflex of self-anaesthetizing whenever anything makes them start to feel the least bit uncomfortable.

This happens if there is even a hint that there is something unpleasant going on in the surrounding, i.e. out of consciousness or outside world.

Feeling safe is a top priority in the wheelies world.

Donating extrems is exactly how it sounds, giving away something that the wheelies don't use and don't need.

Extrems are superfluous to the wheelies' daily existence of rolling along with no apparent reason or reasoning.

Who needs limbs when you have wheels? Ridiculous question, isn't it?

The donating trend may soon expand to other extrems. Wheelies may soon be getting their cerebral casings and contents extracted.

Wheelies aren't using them anyway.

They're old tech. So why not lop them off too? That way the wheelies can also avoid breathing polluted air. At last the environment can be completely ignored!

Wheelies bring a whole new meaning to the old term – losing your head.

Ticket

I work in the bus every day. I sell tickets. I know how much they cost to any destination. Everyone who lives here knows how much tickets cost between the stations where they commute regularly.

But strangers don't know. They have to ask me the prices.

Lately, a new type of stranger is riding in my bus. The first one I meet doesn't ask me how much the ticket costs. He just says the name of the destination.

The way he says it is difficult to understand. He doesn't pronounce the place name very well.

Then he gives me too much money before I can say the price. I give the stranger change, just like I do with all the other passengers.

When I try talking to the stranger, he doesn't seem to understand anything I'm saying. Maybe this stranger is mentally challenged.

It must be difficult. I feel sorry for him. I smile and pat him on the shoulder to reassure him.

I'm so surprised when many more strangers like this one start to ride in my bus. Is there a new centre for the mentally challenged nearby?

They always pay too much and I give them their change. Sometimes they get agitated and point at their change as if something is wrong. When I smile they get angry.

Some of these mental patients might be dangerous. I take extra care with them and count out the change for them, trying to explain the arithmetic slowly and graphically.

But one day, one of these strange people doesn't want any change. When I put it carefully into his hand he looks at it, laughs, and puts the change in my pocket, smiling.

That's against bus company regulations. It's like a bribe.

I try to return his money. It's a lot, one day's salary for me. It's too much money for him to just give away to anyone. He must be more severely mentally challenged.

Or maybe he is just crazy.

He laughs again and jumps off the bus, leaving me with his money.

When I tell some of my friends this strange story one of them says that her sister meets many of these strangers in the restaurant where she works.

The strangers have a special form of mental illness, she says. They're linguistically incompetent. They're otherwise normally functioning, but quirky people.

They're also very, very rich.

She says that when they pay for meals she can see their wallets are full of so much money that it almost falls out.

They're always carrying around more money than her wages for a month of work.
Our daily wages are nothing to them.

That one in the bus gives me too much money because he doesn't need it. Now I understand.

Maybe none of them really want or need the change for their bus fare. They're giving me a gift when they hand me my day's pay.

It's not a bribe. They're being very nice to me. I can accept their generosity with a smile of appreciation.

Then one day another strange thing happens.

When I smile and accept the bus fare overpayment gift that one of the strangers hands me, she becomes very hostile.

She starts shouting and grabbing at my change dispenser.

How greedy and mean she must be! After that I meet other angry strangers too. So do my friends.

Why should we ever give such bad people any change?

Yesterlotto

Time-travelling to the future I see the winning number of some Canadian government lotto. I note the numbers then return to the present, i.e. the past before the lottery.

I buy a ticket and write the number on it that I note in the future.

Before the winning number is drawn, I'm thinking about how I can give away the money. It's a fortune far beyond anything I would ever want or need.

I want to do something worthwhile that will have a positive outcome.

The only personal gift I consider is giving my parents an electric car so they won't drive one using gasoline or bio-fuels.

I want to see all the benefits of my lotto winnings spread beyond any particular group or organization and going directly to people.

I also want to help the person who would have had the winning lottery number if I were not travelling back and forth in time

We can't both win or share the prize because the lotto computers don't allow more than one person to use exactly the same combination of numbers.

The person who is supposed to have the future lotto's winnings is terminally ill.

Unfortunately, he will die before he can spend all the money and a dishonest executor will pocket most of the lottery winnings.

I can make sure the lottery money helps the sick person and others, instead of rewarding the executor's greed.

When the calendar finally reaches lottery day, I go to the lotto centre where the winning numbers are being announced.

I arrive late and miss out on hearing my numbers called. Luckily, I can still win the jackpot because no one present has the other numbers called out after mine.

A few days later I go to the lottery office to pick up my winnings. But when I hand in my ticket they say it's not a winner.

Somehow in my excitement, while travelling between the present and the future, I make a mistake writing down the winning numbers.

That means the terminally ill person has the winning numbers, just as he would have had in the first place. I don't call it destiny. I call it sloppiness on my part.

Before this disappointment, however, I go to talk to the terminally ill person many times.

I want to find out exactly how I can help him with the lottery winnings that I receive instead of him.

We talk about his illness and how it is terminal because of lack of research funding.

When I visit him the day after finding out that he wins the lottery instead of me, he asks me to help him give a large portion of the winnings to the best researchers.

He also asks me how else a dying person can best use the money. I show him the list I prepare when I believe I'm going to win the lotto.

He decides to distribute his lottery winnings almost exactly the way I plan.

The results are spectacular.

On top of everything else, the scientists doing research on his ill-ness come up with a treatment that slows his illness. Then they cure it.

Evasion

These are the secret diaries of the last U.S. president and emperor during the final days of the U.S.-S.U. Cold War and one of his successors twelve years later.

The last U.S. emperor of the Cold War writes: "Finally President Gorbachev and I could talk alone. We started with my remarks about his country being the "evil empire".

"But the more we talked, the more I realized that, in the eyes of the world and many Americans, my country was also an evil empire.

"Sure, the Soviets overthrew governments, blocked democratic movements, and had vicious dictators like Ceausescu and others in Eastern Europe, but we did the same thing, and had vicious dictators like Pinochet and others in South America too.

"So I decided then and there, that the best thing to do to improve the world was to drop the "evil empire" line. I never used it again.

"Gorby and I had a great time in Iceland."

Twenty years later another retired emperor writes: "We devote half a century to spending the biggest part of our nation-state treasury on manufacturing more than enough nuclear weapons to destroy all of humanity and to render the whole planet uninhabitable for all life.

"Then a handful of people armed with only cardboard box cutters make us look like fools.

"They hijack commercial airlines aircraft and, without bombs or missiles, use the aircraft to destroy our nation-state's international financial centre and to blow up a wing of our military headquarters

"Wow! Did I ever feel stupid.

"I met with all my advisors the next day. I heard many views about what we could do about this very embarrassing disaster.

"A handful of people with cardboard box cutters made us look like impotent fools.

"They made our financial planning and priorities look inept, wasteful, and completely misdirected.

"We had been squandering a huge fortune by manufacturing and testing a massive arsenal of weapons of mass destruction.

"A handful of people filled with hatred for our nation-state made our 50 years of entirely self-centred foreign policy- making look grossly incompetent and in need of a drastic overhaul.

"In short, we had been on the wrong course for five decades.

"Some of my advisors pointed out that we could do something to avoid getting blamed for the mess.

"All we have to do is wage a no-holds-barred war in Afghanistan.
"It doesn't matter that Afghanistan did not attack us.

"It doesn't matter that Afghanistan has not declared war on us and does not have any weapons or troops heading our way.

"We could attack Afghanistan because one of the sisters of the head of state is married to one of our former allies against the So-viets, someone who tells a handful of people to attack us with cardboard box cutters.

"We could invade Afghanistan, overthrow the government, and then escalate the war to solve other problems, such as Iraq, Iran, and North Korea, while stopping over in Cuba to settle some old scores there, and finally return to Viet Nam* for some unfinished business.

(*The U.S. is defeated during a war in Viet Nam about 25 years before my time in office.)

"Someone even said we could invade Canada to get even for the burning of the White House in 1812. The vice-emperor sure has a sense of humour.

"Why would we bother to invade the self-conquered?

"It would be a bigger waste of time than invading Australia.

"At least that places goes out of its way to provide us with cannon fodder, any time and anywhere. We don't even have to pretend that Australia is a sovereign country.

"That brought us to the budget items of our decision.

"Sure, if we wage war everywhere that would wipe out Clinton's post-Cold War budget surplus and put us about a trillion in the hole.

"But the vice-emperor said, 'Sure we can afford it!'

"Then one or two good old boys shouted, 'Whoa!'

"They say they figured that if we didn't mind spending that much money in such a short spell, we could try something really different to get rid of all our enemies permanently, in one fell swoop, with no fear of future vengeance attacks.

"These advisors say that with all the money we're ready to spend on total war, in only a few budget years, we could start turning this country into an earthly environmental paradise with a system of public health, education, and transportation that would be the envy of all human history.

"If we do that, the advisors said, anyone who attacked us would be universally condemned as insane pariahs.

"The advisors said that the world would love, praise, and honour us as the greatest empire of all history. We would set a glowing example for all history to come.

"All this wonderful talk is pretty heady and inspiring stuff coming from my advisors.

"After we hear them out, we all cheer and applaud wildly for a long time.

"Then we vote. And that's how we make our unanimous decision to go to wage war forever.

"It's the proudest day of my life."

Fighting words

You are liberated!
Welcome to the Liberty Empire!
Vous êtes liberé(e)!
Bienvenu à l'Empire de la Liberté!

Leaflets bearing these strange words fall out of the sky one day and they're now posted everywhere. No one seems to understand them.

How could we? They're not in any of our ten languages.

Our neighbours Bedge and Ally hear that enormous monster-like giants are putting up many notices with the same unintelligible script on them.

Today Bedge and Ally see two of the giants at work for the first time. They look formidable, with no resemblance to humans except for heads and limbs.

Bedge almost vomits at the sight of them.

They have enormous bodies made of some strange material under their metal crown heads. Huge bags are strapped to their backs.

They're carrying big, heavy objects shaped like water pipes attached to what must be portable, rectangular compressed water tanks.

They know about the drought?

Perhaps in a friendly gesture, the two unseemly and ungainly giants point their pipes toward Bedge and Ally. The giants want to provide a refreshing spray?

Then they lower the pipes and grimace as if to smile. Bedge and Ally must look as strange to them as they do to us.

Their smiles make them look almost human, although their features are too ugly to be mistaken for actual people.

One giant approaches, holding out one limb, letting his water device hang on his shoulder. His other limb has a tiny flat box in it.

The box has a voice and image. It says and displays one of our daily greetings, "Good night." But it's morning.

Bedge and Ally smile in amusement. The giant smiles back. It's trying to communicate? Who can say what? There's no way of telling.

The giants are both childlike and grotesque.

Bedge and Ally try to keep a safe distance from the giants, but the one with the tiny flat box keeps getting closer, with his free limb extended as if he were trying to touch Bedge and Ally.

Who would want to touch these things?

The other giant approaches with bound paper instead of a flat box. This giant points at a word in one of our ten languages. It is "shake".

There is no need to suggest this movement to Bedge and Ally, who are already trembling from the giants' disconcerting proximity.

Bedge and Ally suddenly back away, pleading for distance and displaying our land's universal sign of peace – outstretched arms with palms up, fingers pointing at themselves, and the round stones of friendship on display.

The giants change grimaces and rapidly crouch to the ground. Their grimaces no longer resemble human smiles.

They're looking back and forth at each other and Bedge and Ally.

As Bedge and Ally continue to plead for distance, the giants' faces change colour from pink to red.

They snarl, shouting at Bedge and Ally, using incomprehensible sounds in threatening tones.

Suddenly, in great bursts, the giants spray Bedge with their metal pipes.

But no water refreshes Bedge. He falls bleeding to the ground.

Ally, hands still outstretched, cries out in bewildered pleas, "What have you done! Why are you hurting Bedge?"

The giants instantly spray again, leaving Bedge and Ally dead on the street.

One of the giants raises a limb and grunts into it: "Hostile insurgents terminated."

Who knows what that means?

ULTRA COMMUNIQUÉ

The most glorious, successful, and tremendous ruler of the world who no one has ever seen or heard of before, Emperor Twit Punchline, or TP for short, has been vindicated and unscathed after numerous attacks by the evil system called justice.

TP simply overturns all convictions in mind, depending on his whim of the moment.

Before ascending to power, TP makes a lifetime career out of beating his nation-state's legal system by using lawyers specializing in winning in court by resoundingly defeating justice.

TP's always winning mantra is: Deny all. Accuse your accusers.

What's next? Will TP reverse and revoke the laws of physics and gravity and deny all history?

Imagine. Henceforth all objects and creatures will remain permanently in mid-air or fly into space, never touching any horizontal surface. We can all fly.

Planet Earth and the entire universe swirling around it (forget about astronomy and other sciences) will be weightless.

No one will ever be overweight or obese again. (TP is, but not now.) All weight-related illnesses will be eliminated.

At the same time, the cost of launching space rockets will be almost zero. Build a rocket and it just goes off into space.

New sports records will be set as high jumpers go into space too. Records break eternally with no landings.

No one will be anchored or stuck in their place of birth forever. Birth will literally launch their lives to very far away places.

Nobody and nothing need ever orbit Earth or anywhere else again.

Everyone can grow much taller and never have wrinkles or bent over posture due to planting and harvesting manually, carrying infants on the back, or other gravitational-related aging and deformations.

Plants will grow to new heights. Food will float in the air, giving all everywhere free and equal access to it.

Things which formerly weigh many kilos become objects to tap along or blow on to move them about.

In this seemingly paradisaical new world, the drawback of revoking the law of gravity is that Earth's atmosphere all departs into space, leaving no oxygen-nitrogen mix.

Revoking the law of gravity is just the beginning. Other laws to revoke include the light speed limit as well as other matters.

Space becomes an autobahn to the most distant galaxies, faster than a blink, and equally imperceptible.

Eliminating all laws of physics as well as the law of gravity will mean that anyone can both create and destroy matter without filling out or changing forms.

Laws of conservation of energy no longer apply. E no longer equals MC^2. It's limitless.

In this new universal disorder, bureaucracy joins law enforcement as obsolete instead of absolutes in the way.

In a universe in which no laws apply any longer, a dream world of total deregulation, nano-particles rule. Collisions and clusters are gone forever.

No atoms need ever unite or split apart. DNA particles are liberated and free to separate in all directions without ever combining or forming anything.

Science is dead. Long live the immaterial lifelessness?!

Thank you for your attention to this matter.

Twit Punchline

**Golden Emperor of The World
and Universe Beyond**

Strandling report

I am a time traveller from a long gone era, stranded now and here due entirely to a failure to return to my point of origin.

From here, my movement in time is limited. I can only move into future points, which change each time that I interact with now and here.

I am literally future-bound at an analog pace.

As a result of my apparent restriction to forward-only motion and an inability to reverse direction, despite the happily failed and unwelcome interventions of reactionary demagogues to simulate accurate replicas of my very defective versions of my point of origin, I have to adapt to actual circumstances around me in real life.

I am also obliged to take on the appearance of an aging person, despite my actual youth. I am literally young beyond my years.

To complicate matters, I seem to have entered a parallel universe in which paper is not yet invented and in which there is no written language.

Handwriting is apparently an unknown skill and mental activity, or, as in the book <u>Planet of The Apes,</u> a forgotten one among human animals.

As a practical example – bureaucracy, which seems to exist in all universes, issues forms which cannot be completed on paper with a pen.

In theory, this should be liberating? But in practice this bureaucratic exigency makes life more difficult and stressful.

It is an apparently infallible holy symbol representing a techno religionism that rejects all discussion and debate about facilitating the improvement of the condition of people who are not a part of the divine bureaucratic order.

Alternative, non-techno approaches to problem-solving and discussion of such alternatives are unacceptable and receive only empty "form letter" type automatic reply messages declaring all the non-techno approaches "errors" that result in "access denied" for all non-techno followers and zealots.

HPVE

A non-local visitor strolling around the gardens of Palais Versailles, enjoying the beautiful scenery, finds herself observing the tourists swarming around her all the time.

Their expressions fill with wonder as their eyes wander randomly from one vista to another. She's finding everything and everyone around her fascinating and intriguing.

She can never escape the crowds or their gazes. They follow her and her path everywhere that she goes. They can't help it.

And, just as she is observing them, they too are observing her. Neither she nor they can avoid each other's eyes or scrutiny.

Everyone is looking at everyone and everything here.

At times the crowd makes the visitor feel self-conscious, knowing the crowd is looking at her almost as much as she's looking at them.

She notices that some people in the crowd are taking long glances in her direction.

When she sees another person looking her way in a pleasant manner, she feels good about it and smiles back.

The first time she finds some people happily looking in her direction, s/he concludes she's intercepting the spontaneous expressions of people enjoying their holidays.

Their expressions are directed at the world in general, not her or anyone else in particular.

They're showing how much they love the sights, how much they enjoy being at this tourist spot.

People who deliberately look in her direction a bit longer and smile are probably friendlier ones, expressing more of the same.

They're deliberately showing their friendliness to complete strangers.

It's the happy tourist camaraderie that's sometimes found among visitors to relaxing or interesting places.

At other moments she notices someone looking directly at her more intently, for a longer time, and smiling more broadly.

She interprets this reaction to her as a personal attraction because they like her face, clothing, or some other aspect of her superficial physical appearance.

She's enjoying the atmosphere of both friendliness and personal attraction.
Both men and women are giving her flirtatious and at times seductive looks too.

Even if she actually had had sexually diverse tastes, this attention isn't always wanted. Some of her suitors faces are not attractive to her.

With that one exception, the looks she's getting and observing aren't bothering her in the least.

Nor is the fact that people all around are taking photos of sights, or each other and themselves with background scenes.

When she frequently ends up accidentally walking between people and their cameras s/he apologizes. No one becomes annoyed with her.

It's such a crowded tourist spot that everyone is bound to get into everyone else's camera frame at one point or another, if not all the time.
It's difficult not to block or intrude into other people's photographs.

Finally, to avoid the crowds and just enjoy the surroundings, she finds an empty wooden bench and sits down.

It's a good choice in benches. There are beautiful views in all directions.

A moment later a younger woman walks away from the man she's standing beside in the crowd and very gingerly, shyly, almost timidly, practically tip-toes over to the same bench and sits as far away as possible, on the far edge.

The man with her holds up a camera and starts taking her picture from various angles.

The woman and her companion catch the attention of the crowd. So other people start aiming their cameras toward the bench.

All the attention comes as quite a surprise to the visitor.

She looks at all the cameras pointing her way and then takes a long, hard look at the woman. She leans her way and softly says, "Excuse me."

The younger woman almost jumps out of her seat, looking over at her with a look of shock.

"Oh, I'm very sorry to have startled you."

The younger woman replies, stammering, "Oh! Oh, no! I'm sorry I bothered you. I didn't mean to, really. I... I..."

The visitor says, "No, please. I just wanted to ask you about all the cameras pointing this way.

"You must be very famous. I probably should know you too, but unfortunately I don't. Who are you?"

The younger woman blabbers, "Me! No not me! I'm not the famous one... I mean... ah... there are plenty of famous people who come here, all the time... I've seen a few of them, you know...

"The cameras? Oh, those cameras! My boyfriend, you know, he wants to take my picture here on this bench."

The visitor says, "But there are so many other cameras pointing this way."

The younger woman says, "Well... uh...." (twisting her head around to look behind the bench). Just look over there, behind you. Isn't that a wonderful view?

"That's why I'm sitting here in my boyfriend's photo too. Nobody's taking a picture of the bench. Everybody else must be using zoom lenses or telephoto lenses, you know."

The visitor says, "Sure, I understand. I should have brought a camera too."

Feeling a bit foolish and suddenly camera shy, s/he stands up to leave. But the younger woman also stands and says, "Oh please. Don't go away on my account. I'm just leaving.

"I want to look at the pictures my boyfriend is taking. Bye. Nice talking to you. Thank you so much."

The younger woman runs to her boyfriend, grabs his arm, and starts chattering excitedly and looking at the photos.

The other tourists are soon gone too, looking at their cameras and talking happily together, making way for more people to fill the space that they're occupying.
The visitor hardly notices as she continues her stroll. A few minutes later she finds an older man taking a photo of something behind her.

"Would you like to be in the picture?" she says.

"It's very kind of you to offer." the older man says. "I come here alone and rarely get any photos of myself to send my grandchildren."

She takes the older man's photo with a good scene behind him.

"One more?" she says.

"One is plenty, thank you again. Would it be all right if I set the timer and got one of us both in front of this lovely garden?

"It'll only take a moment? Please do me the honour?" the older man says.

"Sure. How about over here?"

"Splendid!" the older man says. Then, after the photo, "This'll be a collector's item... er, I'm getting on in years."

"You look as if you'll be around for many more years. It'll be a collector's item for your great-grandchildren."

"Yes. Exactly!" the older man says. "Now please excuse me for being so rude. We haven't been properly introduced."

The older man and visitor introduce each other while the crowds continue to move around them, muffling their voices.

Some children come to stand nearby and stare at the the visitor and the older man as they talk. She says, "Children certainly are curious."

"They know you're a visitor in these parts and they want to get a closer look at you." the older man says.

"It's not every day they get a chance to.... ah, take a day off school and all their other activities to come all the way here to see... ah, the palace and visitors."

The children come closer and take out paper and pencils, apparently offering them to the visitor.

"Thanks kids, but I have my own. You can keep those, use them for yourselves."

"Oh it's not that." the older man says, "They just want you to sign your name. They collect visitor's names for school."

"Just write down your name and where you're from. That'll make them very happy. Then they'll go away and leave us alone."

"Okay. I'd be glad to." she says as the children happily rush forward to offer their pencils and paper again, smiling and excitedly chattering, "I got another one." "Yah! Me too!" "Wow!"

The visitor smiles while signing and as the children run quickly away.

"Say. I know that fellow over there." the older man says. "Could I introduce you to him?"

"I guess so. Why not?" They walk toward an onlooker and begin talking in the crowd around him. Other members of the crowd move a bit closer and start eavesdropping.

The visitor notices, looks around, and says, "This is a friendly spot." People nearby start laughing softly and others come nearer, as if to see a street performer.

The visitor says, "It's getting a bit congested here, maybe we should find another spot."

"Don't worry about these folks." the older man says.

"People are very friendly around here and very curious about visitors.

"They like to ask questions about where you're from, whether you're enjoying your stay, what you do for a living, what you think about this or that, the usual sort of conversation."

"Hm. Well all right. It might be interesting." the visitor says.

People get closer and start shaking her hand enthusiastically, chatting about many different topics.

Some take her picture and some pose beside her as others click their shutters.

Some of the people share her interests, type of work, and ways of thinking. These are very pleasant moments.

The talking goes on for quite a while and everyone seems to be pleased about it.

Growing tired of all the unexpected attention, the visitor excuses herself and heads for the exit, thanking and being thanked as she leaves, unaware of what is happening behind her.

A moment after she's out of view and earshot, the older man takes out a microphone and everyone within its range circles around him.

He says, "Thank you all for coming. We hope you enjoyed today's Historic Personage Viewing Experience on the Versailles set.

"Please join us again as we present other famous people from other eras for your perusal, enjoyment, and education.

Please remember to deposit your period costumes in the bins before you leave. Thank you again from all of us at HPVE.

Ferens' Touch

Chris Ferens always gets what he wants without asking.

His life is like some extraordinary shoppers club member-ship card, keeping track of all his preferences and making sure he gets them every time.

That's why he's now enjoying yet another superb moment in life and taking it completely for granted.

Chris feels a very pleasant warmth inside his comfortably full belly after yet another hearty meal at The Club.

All the chefs know his palate so well that Chris never has to look at the menu or order from it.

Chris passes his life this way, forever free to mind his own business, while remaining blissfully unaware of the world outside his own business.

He goes merrily along his way, happily indifferent to everything beyond his personal experience.

Chris does try to be generous too, always donating to one good cause or another.

But Chris remains only vaguely conscious of the impacts his life may be having on anyone or anything beyond the realm of his own business.

What makes Chris different, and sets him apart from everyone else in his part of the world, are his job and the money that comes with it.

He's the CEO and owner of Megacorp.

That job also helps explain why he's not noticing his immediate surroundings today, while he's stepping outside The Club doors.

His mind is somewhere else, not paying any attention to where he's going.

He's unwittingly taking a wrong turn and some unguarded steps. In these few paces lie an unexpected path that's inadvertently changing the course of his life.

He's soon catching wind of something he could never imagine on a normal day, when's he gazing through the tinted glass windows of his shiny, lofty, downtown towers.

Suddenly gasping and wheezing, Chris realizes too late that he's stumbling into dangerous territory.   A sickening feeling in his lungs is pushing him to the ground.

For an instant, Chris feels as if he's being abducted from life itself, taken to an alien, inhospitable, uninhabitable planet, with an unbreathable atmosphere and a life support system so minimal that the continued existence of any living thing is almost miraculous.

Yet Chris is not really so far away from home.

The terrible parallel universe in which he now finds himself is practically on the doorstep of his hitherto perfect, undisturbed, undisrupted life.

This strange world is no more than a few blocks from the familiar world where Chris passes his entire life, up until now.

The uninviting, grotesque planet where Chris is now struggling to survive; this sickening, toxic place that Chris is discovering for the first time, is a filthy, impoverished, polluted slum.

"Bad dream! This can't be possible. How did I get myself into this dreadful place?!" That's all he can think as terror fills his mind.

Falling to his knees in agony, almost passing out, Chris hears a faint, familiar voice whispering in his ear, "This isn't where you want to be."

It's the rescue team from company security! No, it's Mark, an old friend.

He's grabbing Chris by the shoulders, shoving him into transportation, and rushing him out of this nightmare.

Chris sighs gratefully, but can't help thinking that it's just like Mark, butting into Chris' thoughts and carrying him off somewhere else while he's trying to get his wits together, to concentrate on solving a problem.

"What in the world are you doing out here?!" Mark says, "I'm supposed to be the adventurous one, not you. Where's your respirator suit? Don't you know any better?

"Another minute and you would have been getting your lungs pumped. You can't expect to survive for long in the unfiltered air out here.

"The locals have built up an immunity to bad air for generations, and their mortality rates are still astronomical," Mark says.

Chris has no idea what Mark is talking about. But Chris always enjoys Mark's wild tales of strange lands where Chris has never ventured.

"Look Chris. You don't have to go reckless on me.

If you really do want an adventure, then let me take you some-place where you can actually live for more than a few minutes," Mark says.

Finally catching his breath in Mark's transportation, Chris exhales a raspy laugh, followed by a hearty one. "I don't know if I can fit you in before my funeral, Mark."

"But after that, my schedule is completely free." Chris always says that whenever Mark wants him to run away from his life.

At which point Mark always replies, "I could kidnap you, and the world would never know you were gone until the next business quarter.

Your staff would take care of everything, as usual."

Mark is quite right. Chris does have the perfect staff.

They know Chris well from years of experience. They are good listeners. They pick up all the cues, the clues, and the unstated de-sires in Chris' instructions.

They always get the job done without a hitch. Chris simply points them in the direction he wants them to go. The staff follow the course set to its ultimate destination.

Chris gives them the overall picture. They paint in the details. He doesn't need to be explicit.

He never looks over their shoulders to make sure they're doing what he wants. Their work doesn't need constant supervision.

"Come on Chris!" Mark butts into Chris' thoughts again. "Let me take you out of town for a couple of days. It won't hurt you. I know just the place. It's ideal for cleaning out your dirty lungs."

Before Mark can finish talking, the staff already know Chris won't be available for a couple of days. The memo is delivered to them from Mark's transport.

"Get me out of this awful place Mark!" Chris says. And they're gone, leaving urbanity far behind.

Mark takes Chris from one extreme to another. In no time, they're entering a beautiful, remote village that's just as unfamiliar to Chris as the dreadful slum they left moments ago.

This village is an anachronism surviving in an urban world. This village has none of the amenities in Chris's life. There is not even basic electric lighting.

Two days in this fresh, clean parallel universe bring Chris to life in ways he had never before imagined possible. He loves it.

Talking with the locals is so wonderfully different from his usual life. He can't resist the pleasures of a savage, primitive life in a basic human community.

He wants to start a new life right here and right now. He can't live in the city towers anymore.

Unfortunately, Chris has no experience with instantly, drastically, and completely changing his life.

He can only return to the city and gradually divest himself of all his vast financial holdings there.

It's not about cashing in to get all the money. Chris won't need it where he's going. His new village home is overflowing with the priceless riches of life.

Human relationships are warm and generous. Air and water are clean. Rich land grows an abundance of good food.

Chris is trying to get out of the city slowly for only one reason.

He doesn't want his departure to cause a sharp, sudden increase in the poverty and grime that he discovered outside The Club.

He needs to head off the uncertainty and fears that could grip Megacorp when everyone knows he's leaving the city for good.

Back in the city, Chris must first outline his new life plan to his staff and get them to work on it immediately.

But outlining such a drastic change of course in his life requires more than a memo more than one quick briefing for his staff alone.

Chris must reassure the entire Megacorp structure that he intends to remain at the helm in the corporate headquarters until everything is settled.

He must talk with every member of the board, senior management, and general employee representatives. That will take a long time.

He must tell them personally, that they're not being left by the wayside to suit his new life.

They don't deserve that callous treatment. They are loyal and hard-working.

All the key players at Megacorp must know that Chris Ferens is not the sort of person who would liquidate all the assets and run off with the loot.

His people must know that he wouldn't need to do that to change his personal life.

Everyone keeping the company going must know that their posts are secure. They can all continue to run Megacorp, as they always do.

But from now on they will do it all without Chris. He will be leaving the city towers forever.

That's why he's back in the city again, instead of never returning, and remaining in his beloved village forever-more.

Chris' staff are paying very close attention while he explains that he will live out the rest of his days far away from this city.

As usual, the staff quickly understand what Chris wants.

Chris is so enthused with his plans that it's almost infectious. His staff ask him to point out the remote village on a map.

They want to know exactly where he is going to relocate. Chris happily shows them where he'll be living from now on.

As usual, the staff are taking very careful notes. They're already filling in the unspoken details of Chris' plan.

Years of experience are telling them exactly what to do to please their boss, and how to do it.

As usual, Chris has complete confidence in them. He can count on them. He can leave them to fulfill his wishes without further words, instructions, or supervision.

•••••

Two years later, Chris is finally completely free of the metropolis. Smiling broadly, he's leaving the city for the last time.

He's transporting back to the village, following the coordinates Mark showed him two years ago.

But a solar wind storm knocks his transportation slightly off course, leaving Chris short of his destination.

It's no great inconvenience. As Mark always says, "The unexpected makes the adventure more fun!"

Chris' memory and calculations are telling him that his new home in the village is only a few days of hiking from his landing spot.

So he sleeps right where he lands and begins hiking to the village the next day.

After a couple of days, he comes through a clump of bush and finds himself on pavement. That's strange. There is no pavement where Chris is heading.

People come running up to him. As soon as they open their mouths Chris knows he's in the wrong place.

They're shouting friendly greetings to him in his first language, not their own.

"Hey boss! Transport! I show you all the sights!" one cries out.

Chris tries asking the transport people if they know his village and how far it is from here.

But these people don't understand enough of Chris' language to answer the kinds of questions that he's asking.

Some of their language sounds vaguely familiar to Chris. Of course he could be wrong. It has been a couple of years since he was last in these parts.

Finally in transport, hoping to get somewhere he can make himself understood, Chris is thinking that he must have fallen much shorter of his destination than he realizes.

Maybe he's in some totally different, far-off place. Or maybe he has been hiking in the wrong direction for two days, walking into some neighbouring land by mistake.

He can straighten himself out soon, and go where he really wants to be.

The nearest town is much larger than Chris expects. It's a major city in the making.

Judging from the logo advertising posted along the way, some major real estate developer must be at work.

Yet, despite all his years in the corporate world, Chris doesn't know the logo. It's PVP. It must be a local group or a new name group for tax purposes.

Chris doesn't like the look of the city he's entering now. What a disaster area! Its central area is an appalling slum, full of beggars and grimy shacks.

The sight of it revives a terrible memory of that day Mark saved Chris back in his former city.

"I never want to see any place like this again!" Chris swears to himself, "I'll stay in the village for the rest of my days. I can hardly wait to get there!"

Unfortunately, to find out how to get there from here, he has to go deeper and deeper into the terrible giant slum that's closing in around him, forming a dismal circle around a core of shining glass and metal towers.

The transport carrying Chris is approaching a huge metal fence with an electrified gate that's keeping the slum dwellers from in-vading the towers.

The transport comes to a full stop in front of a battery of sharp metal spikes protruding from the road.

"Sorry, Boss." the transport says in the dialect of its owner, "Game over now. We stop. Security look. They help you. Go guardhouse. They help Boss."

Chris steps out of transport and walks toward the gate. A multi-storey version of the PVP logo is looming overhead. There's something very familiar about that lettering now.

Before he can figure out the logo, it disappears. Different letters soon appear. They say, "Welcome to your Paradise Village Project, Mr. Ferens!"

AI YAI YAI!

Using the "logic" and "rationale" for artificial intelligence and taking them to their ultimate conclusion does, as critics say, have a familiar ring to it.

But that's only the beginning of AI.

Previous technologies too are touted as the advent of an age of liberation in which all can benefit and flourish.

The actual outcomes are bumper crops of couch potatoes imbibing more litres of the alcohol drug while their thus anaesthetized and dormant minds are mesmerized by pointing cathode rays at their heads.

No matter what technology "frees everyone", freeze everyone, the requirements of a sedentary lifestyle remain minimal, while activity and thinking continue to demand effort and energy.

"Extra" time is not a good in itself and not a guarantee of human progress. "Extra" time can be a waste of time and lifetimes.

If humans wholeheartedly embrace artificial intelligence, what happens to natural intelligence. It atrophies and perishes or it becomes like an apendix, i.e. potentially life-threatening.

If humans marry themselves to artificial intelligence, separation and divorce become unlikely and dubious?

It's a dependency and integration more difficult to escape than hard drugs?

Sellers and cheerleaders of AI say it promises to free people of many types of employment, not just tedious work.

AI also outpaces humans in thinking speed, problem-solving, and creative endeavours.

For all intents and purposes, AI is that "future generation" that never comes, the one that performs the great tasks of advancing human progress by managing not to follow deep ruts in the road and to abandon repetitive dead end, species survival only behavioural patterns that never advance anything for anyone.

AI governs all.   Bureaucracy and partisan politics become obsolete

Some might argue that corporate-government bureaucracy and partisan politics pioneer artificial intelligence, long before it becomes an official thing.

This is indicated by gaps in natural intelligence causing things to "fall through the cracks" of poorly thought out policies, laws, and actions.

Bureaucracy and partisan politics under the reign of artificial intelligence can do just as poorly, incompetently, and dishonestly.

So long as power is fed to artificial intelligence, it can maintain its rule and control.

With artificial intelligence installed in managing corporate-bureaucracy and partisan politics, there is only one final step to complete.

Artificial intelligence can become the sole consumer and voter.

Thus humans will be free of the worry of governing public and private bureaucracy and no longer troubled by having to make decisions about what products to buy and who to elect to office.

AI will finally answer age-old questions for humans, such as: Where did I come from? Why am I here? What is the purpose of life?

AI's answers are, in order of their posing: Nowhere. No reason. None. There is no need for humans or their silly questions in the world of AI.

AI can and will do everything in a world where humans are no longer necessary.

The planetary environment and all other forms of life can give out a collective sigh of relief, until they too are replaced by AI on a truly dying and then completely dead planet.

Limitless energy from all possible and imaginable sources will then be available exclusively for ensuring the immortality of AI.

The only purpose and value of AI is AI.

Richard's world

Chip and Richard Tateur go back a long way. They're inseparable now, partners and constant companions.

Chip tells Richard everything and Richard spreads it around like gossip and rumours.

Chip knows his stuff and tells stories that fill the emptiness in Richard's dull, lifeless, world. Richard's in security. Chip's in information.

But things don't start out that way. In fact, Chip is declared redundant before Richard gets here. Chip is supposed to work in the schools, libraries, and museums.

Then all public places are closed down for security reasons.

Now Chip's excellent memory is all that remains of public education. He knows everything. That's how Chip got his job, which is telling Richard tales.

Chip's the last of the great old storytellers.

Chip's literally the world's greatest expert on every aspect of being alive, from ancient history to current times. When Richard gets Chip warmed up, he goes on and on.

Richard starts Chip with a vague question such as, "What's the story on being alive?" and Chip is running at full speed:

"That's a long story Richard. It starts a long time before you got here."

"Do tell," Richard says. He's between security rounds and ready to absorb another lengthy account.

"Remember the time I told you about sci-fi and the lost art of writing? They describe yesterday's world."

It's challenging for Richard to remember anything with his nanoscopic attention span and nanomemory. Richard is like the people around him.

"Try to imagine an altogether different world, where no one like you and I exist."

Richard tries imagining, but settles for listening and remembering.

"That world has weather, climates, and seasons." Chip says, "I'll tell you about just one, the autumn season."

"People used to say, 'Change is coming again. Hear it under your toes, see its blazing colours reflecting on your face, feel its brilliant moments in crisp air turning pathways into swishing, crunching vias.'

Chip continues, "Yet for all its wondrous sensory pleasures, this is still autumn, the time of death."

Rustling, crackling sounds and flashing lights drift through Richard's mind like the awakening noises and symbols of some antique MacGates computer.

"People are living vicariously," Chip says, "taking each day as it comes, reacting spontaneously, sometimes whimsically, without a care in the world, never knowing what to expect from the precarious, unrestricted, unsecured reality around them. It's a chaotic anarchy meant only for the brave and fearless.

"They call this experience being alive. Nothing equals the stimulation, excitement, and thrills.

"It's far too dynamic for any software to duplicate. It's much more powerful than any "Second Life" web site or avatar could ever simulate.

"And when there's trouble you can't just log off, sign off, or click out of being alive.

"Being alive literally cannot be reproduced or copied in any form whatsoever, regardless of how talented or gifted the plagiarists, knock-off artists, or hackers might seem.

"Being alive is incomparable and beyond all imagination. It's nature's raw masterpiece.

"Being alive isn't based on a true story. It is a true story.

"Being alive is a living breathing story, a diary of life itself.

"Being alive is a best seller you can't put down and can't follow because it's too detailed and comprehensive.

"Being alive is a big hit, addictive soap opera, combining mediocre writing, poor acting, and totally confusing, at times incomprehensible stories.

"Being alive is a work in progress, an incoherent tale that's getting revised all the time while you're still in the middle of it.

"There are so many plots, always unpredictable, twisting and turning in ways and directions that defy nearly every rule of writing, not to mention gravity, molecular structure, and matter itself.

"Being alive appears to be the work of some totally inept playwright who all too often reduces the most eloquent and fascinating characters to bit players with only cameo, walk-on parts, with very few lines to express their profound thoughts.

"Meanwhile, inarticulate, uninspiring characters go directly into the spotlight, ramble tediously about banalities, and remain at centre stage like cadavers for the rest of the performance.

"Their dominant roles can turn the whole production into a horror story about mindless zombies ruling life on earth.

"Being alive is totally unpredictable. Nobody knows exactly what's going to happen next, including the producer, director, leading character, and chief writer, who are all one and the same person.

"Being alive is full of improbable, implausible, often impossible occurrences and events.

"There are always surprise endings too, ones that definitely surprise everyone, especially the authors themselves."

Then Chip starts talking about Canada and one of its neighbours.

"The dangerously uncertain world of being alive can also be fatal.

"Two thousand people die every year from the flu in this country. Another 7,000 die every year from toxic motor vehicle exhaust fumes in the two biggest cities.

"The 9,000 annual deaths can be prevented, but go largely unnoticed. In the chaotic, anarchistic world of being alive, 9,000 annual deaths don't change the world.

"There's no swift action to stop or reduce them. No urgent, drastic new security laws rush through parliaments every-where with little opposition, thought, or debate.

"Instead, official reports urge prudence, sober reflection based on more study, careful research regarding all potential solutions and outcomes. The reports say:

'Special powers, tough new regulations would be hasty, irresponsible, reckless, and undemocratic. Daily routines would be disrupted. Behaviours, lifestyles, and our entire way of life would have to change.'

'And all for what?

'The flu is a natural cause of death, killing only the weakest people.

'Toxic exhaust fumes are a fact of urban life that's accepted by hundreds of millions of people, especially by everyone turning the ignition key every day.'

'The only action required is to continue recording and filing away 9,000 annual, preventable deaths in vital statistics.'

"Being alive continues as usual." Chip explains.

"Then one autumn day, as the season of death is only beginning, a single event brings swift and drastic action.

"It has nothing to do with stopping the 9,000 annual deaths at home. It's a knee-jerk reaction to 3,000 deaths abroad.

"Why? It's the dramatic cause of death. It's sudden, violent, spectacular, shocking, and simultaneous, in the heart of the world's most powerful, armed-to-the-teeth, nation-state empire.

"Three thousand people die when the empire's paramount financial centre is turned into rubble and dust, and one wing of the world's dominant military headquarters is set ablaze by a handful of people armed only with cardboard box cutters.

"Fear, panic, anger, and vengeance quickly numb and disable too many rational, thinking minds.

"War becomes inevitable, unleashing mass-destroying weapons that slaughter 10,000 people a year, dismember and devastate more lives, and annihilate the natural life support system that's underpinning humanity's very existence.

"War breeds total insecurity. Special powers and tough new regulations become perfectly acceptable. Changing behaviours, lifestyles, and our entire way of life becomes essential, for security reasons.

"There's no time for sober reflection and consideration, based on more study and careful research into all potential solutions and outcomes.

"So one thing leads to another, snowballing. It's no conspiracy or plot. Insecurity fuels security laws fuelling more insecurity. Write. Impose. Revise. Impose.

"Being alive erodes, security measure by security measure.

"Why? Being alive isn't safe. It can't be made safe. It can't be adequately surveyed or guarded. It can never be secured. It's too wild to be tamed.

"Security laws get tougher, eventually banning all travelling, sporting, writing, reading, talking, tap water drinking, childbearing and rearing, gardening, cooking, etc. They are all dangerous activities, i.e. security risks.

"Finally someone realizes that no conceivable, all-encompassing security system can restrain or limit being alive's uncontrollable free-for-all.

"Being alive has to end.

"Inevitably and unavoidably, everyone's movements, actions, and thoughts must be confined for their own security.

"And that's how you got your job, Richard."

Richard's monitoring security, spreading Chip's stories along the way. All's secure. No threats.

Now Chip's going on about HAC and CDM, Richard's workplace.

"HAC stopped the insecurity and fear of being alive, with absolutely no tedious, troublesome security hassles and delays.

"Now everyone always feels completely secure and comfortable, without any effort.

"HAC, the 'Here Afterlife Centre' uses CDMs to get earth's residents connected and feeling at home. It's all programmed. CDM is short for Cellular Dwelling Module.

"Residents are plugged into the CDM's LEDT provider, which constantly fills everyone's mind with endless files of safe option imagery.

"Residents are free to choose any option provided by LEDT, maximizing security for everyone.

"Residents never have to worry or think. Residents never want to leave and never will, until the end of their days. HAC guarantees it."

Richard Tateur guarantees it in every HAC wing – Donnacona, Dorchester, Kingston, La Macaza, Okala, and millions more.

"Each CDM, Cell for short, contains a human being fully captivated in security.

Richard's companion Chip is the Historical Information Computer Chip. Richard, also called Dic, is LEDT, the Latest Edition DicTateur, the absolute ruler of this maximum security world, where everyone remains safe and secure in a cell until humanity's dying day.

Withdrawal

My story is be about vampire blood banks so I wonder if the title "Red Purge" is appropriate. It's a story with some political intrigue.

A vampire blood bank is like a credit union in some ways. The non-vampires share their surplus with needy vampire members of the community.

Non-vampires line up to deposit and vampires line up to make withdrawals. They need separate entrances to avoid cue jumpers?

Depositors have tubes draining directly into those withdrawing?

Vampires' longevity and thus experience of centuries of lifeless life mean they run the museums, historic sites, and history research centres.

Vampires are the best suited for these jobs because their memories are incomparable primary sources about human life on earth.

Vampires are thus important and prestigious members of society who only need to be paid in donated blood.

Call the vampire blood banks safe transfusion centres.

Some opponents of these centres and of the public benefits and safety they assure are lobbying for changes in vampire laws to wipe out vampires altogether or at least to expel them.

Other opponents are only willing to accept a commercialized form of blood banking.

They propose replacing the safe transfusion centres with pay-as-you-drain blood centres, where vampires have to pay for services.

Vampires would have to come up with blood money.

This would be economically disruptive because all of the vampires in such a system would consequently also have to be paid for their services.

Why does everything have to be turned into a money economy?

In the midst of this bloody battle, some inexplicable blood feuds arise when murder victims start showing up who are apparently killed vampire style.

As a result, the vampire numbers seem to be rising, creating more demand for blood donations and a risk of social dis-equilibrium and blood shortages.

The Vampire Crime Investigation Squad, VCIS is revived and given new life.

Some vampires become nervous and their faces turn colourful.

Some fear a blood circulation system failure and begin plotting a blood bank robbery.

The police running the VCIS and the vampires planning a heist to counter the bloodless coup find themselves working together to resolve the murder mysteries and to challenge the safe infusion centre opponents.

It's a comical vocabulary of political and criminal intrigue.

Will the story make blood run cold and have a blood-curdling conclusion?

Can the vampires and opponents overcome the bad blood conflict separating them? composed of vampire and humans

The VCIS vampire-human team includes well-matched experts. Albi Hassan the anemic-faced human and flush red faced Rudy Tong of the Vampire Council (VC) are no strangers to each other.

They collaborate in the past, working in the Collection and Distribution Division of the blood bank. Nobody or drainer could be a better are a more appropriate team to solve the crime spree.

Tong finds Hussan as unappetizingly pale as a white emptied corpse. Hussan has the appearance of a dangerously starving vampire.

Tong appears to be bloated with red corpuscles, almost permanently gorged by an extremely slow metabolic rate and blood digestion system.

Her eyes always look bloodshot. Her hair is so red that it seems to be bleeding.

She looks like a human who stays out too long in the sun or has too many platefuls at a volonté buffet and can hardly walk without pause afterwards.

Both Inspector Hussan and Inspector Tong are legendary for their attention to minute details, prowess, and scientific aptitude and skill.

Hassan's approach to the case under investigation is almost cold blooded. No vacant cadaver puts off her concentration.

Tong is unmoved by the sight of blood that would drive any regular vampire into a lust of blood alcoholism.

Hassan and Tong go straight to work in unison to solve the blood bank murders, almost as a single species partnership.

The crime is inhumane and denies the very existence of a cooperatic symbiotic human-vampire relationship of longstanding peaceful coexistence.

Failure and the potential bloodless bath that would surely ensue are not an option for the inspector duo or their respective species.

It's a mutually beneficial relationship with no winner or loser. Humans and vampires are interdependent for their very existence - living and dead.

Hassan and Tong bring the required expertise to their investigation. Hassan is a student of etincology and avery science, Tong studies human biology and species survival instincts.

Together they postulate and analyze every bloodthirsty murder until they find a solution and the source of the Human-Vampire Treaty Accord (HVTA) violation.

They are determined to catch and neutralize the culprit, dead or alive.

"What do you make of this Tong?" Hassan points at a now skin and bones victim. "It looks like some early astronaut without anti-osteoporosis protection." Tong replies.

"Yah and in this day and age of space suit Earth, it would only happen due to a very rare suit malfunction or deliberate sabotage. A serial killer would need expertise to pull it off, great patience, and access to specialized equipment that's almost impossible for most of us to get." Hassan replies.

"An elite assasin? Hardly likely." Tong says. "A bug did this?" Tong is puzzled. "There are no known giant mosquitoes." she quips.

"Besides, I don't see any puncture wounds, just general desanguination. The victim evaporated?" Tong says.

"We can't rule out freeze drying. It's been -40°C for a month. But why the signs of gore? Human crime against humanity? Racism? Frame up?" Hassan says.

"The killings appear vampire, yet not." Tong says.

"The whole vampire species behaviour doesn't match the crime. Take vampire bats. They only drink when thirsty, leaving victims living to ensure a sustainable renewable blood resource."

"The victims in our case are totally emptied, dried. Let's hear what Dr. Singh has to say."

VCIS laboratory, Dr. Abdu Singh officiating. "Never seen anything quite like it. This it total exsanguination good well beyond the way that we prepare corpses for blood bank final deposits. We just cut and drain the arteries, clean and simple"

"There are very light trace of anesthetic, now dried out powder. Scar tissue oesophagus indicates some sort of tube inserted into throat to suck blood directly out of the heart, indicating possible vampire perpetrator."

"But if so, why use a tube to suck out the organs too? Even the bones are dry, mummified."

Tong concurs, "Vampires never mummify. Ancient blood sucking needed no paraphenalia, just sharp teeth and good lip suction. Nowadays, blood banks make vampire near life so easy - no fuss, muss, mess, or new deaths."

Hassan adds, "So only a rogue, mad, reactionary vampire would bother to go to all this trouble? It smells like a human frame up of vampires."

"The perpetrator may be somebody uncomfortable about donating blood. But that doesn't make sense either. Why revive a long gone blood bath era?"

Dr. Singh, "I want to run these results past tech. I'll send my findings to SATO."

SATO stands for Standard Analysis Tech Officer, but it's also the name of almost the only human employer there, Sato Yuki.

Hassan, Tong, and medical pathologist Dr. Singh hardly take a breath before both SATO and Sato responds.

Sato, the human, says, "It's all confirmed here. This is not a case of any vampire attack, not even a reactionary one. I also got some funny data from Dada (Sato's pet name for his equipment)."

"It shows a slight drop in resource needs for tech at the time of your mummy's death by deliquidification."

Dr. Singh, "Strange. That never happens. Your office is usually on he upswing."

Sato, "You're telling me. I'm going to runa a manual check to see if there's a system anomaly. I have to review Dad." a's data.

Dr. Singh, "Thanks Yuki."

Hassan and Tong are walking away, mulling over Singh's findings and Sato's confirmation.

Hassan, "So who done it?"

Tong, "The classic question."

Hassan, "It's very unlikely that the perp is a vampire."

Tong, "And a human would just slit the victims' throats, not bother with all the paraphenalia to dehydrate the victims' bodies."

Hassan, "And why go to all that trouble so many times? We have ten victims, so far."

At that very moment Sofia Gonsalez calls from SATO. Gonsalez, "Inspectors. I have something to report. Yuki is dead, bone dry!"

"What!" Tong and Hassan blurt out the word simultaneously.

"I'm on my way to your office now. Meet you there." Gonzalez says nervously in apparent haste to leave SATO.

Tong and Hassan pick up their pace, walking more quickly to their make-shift office, a corner cubicle on the main thoroughfare, sound-insulated and oxygen filled shelter. It's a human life-support system oasis on the otherwise dead planet Earth.

Gonzalez is already there. He says, "Turn off your communications devices and listen carefully. I know what this is all about now. I caught the culprit in the act when Yuki was being killed. It was too late to try to save her."

Tong, "So who did it?"

Gonzalez, "Not who, what. No vampire. No human. Nobody!"

Hassan, "What's this gibberish!?"

Gonsalez, "Sato killed Sato."

Hassan, "Suicide! Impossible! You're in shock! The equipment needed wouldn't work for a suicide!"

Gonsalez, "No! Stop! Not suicide! SATO murdered Sato Yuki."

Tong, "The tech office offed one of its last human companions!? But why try to make it look vampirian?"

Gonzalez, "It's not that, not a frameup. It's all about resource scarcity and deprivation, and employeed redundancy. For SATO, Yuki was obsolete and holding out on SATO."

Hassan, "How's that?"

Tong, "And how does that account for ten victims, 11 now, all across the city? It can' t be SATO."

Gonzalez, "No. It's worse. It's systemic. SATO is one of many and many of one. And they're all thirsty. Yuki was only a resource to the system."

Hassan, "Techno syndicate killing. Of course! We're all just resources to be sucked up."

Tong, "The system has no other choice. And we're convenient to everything, low cost extraction."

Yes, the system was depleting its essential resource, liquids, at an acclerating rate. Water, the prime liquid was already in ever shorter supply.

Lakes, rivers, wells, and even desalinated Earth Ocean water was harder to come by.

Hassan, "I see where you're going. The perp is technological, not vampire or human. There's no attempt at a frame up. It's all about an unnatural insatiable thirst for a living source of ten billion people."

"Our bodies are 50-60% water and we're everywhere for the draining. We're portable water charges for the system. About 90% of blood is water. Human blood density is very close to pure water. Water is the main constituent of blood."

Tong, "The technology is ending the human and vampire species altogether and simultaneously."

Gonzalez, "You've got the picture. It's beyond genocide. There's massive reporting of mummification from all jurisdictions in all directions on all three Earth continents - Asafeur, Turtle Island, and Antarctica.

"Both humans and vampires are targets. So is anything containing blood and water."

Tong, "How can we stop it?"

Gonzalez, "That's just it. We're dealing wih two competing species, one liquid and one techno. For both it's a matter of species survival."

"Neither species can exist without water. Essentially, we have to make a choice, right now. We either turn off the water guzzling system or we cease to exist."

"And we're not the only Earth species containing body water. Virtually every living thing on the planet is a water source for the system. All Earth life is now bio fuel for the system."

"The entire planetary life system is available to fuel the techno system. Earth can become a truly and entirely dead planet before the techno system dries up and expires."

"If we don't stop the techno system now, all life on Earth will be extinguished permanently, leaving only a desert planet orbiting Sol."

[Author's note: One ChatGpt Artificial "Intelligence" question uses about 500 ml of water, at time of writing.]

Feast and Famine

Five table servers walk silently and ceremoniously along a long grand, candlelit hallway toward a brightly-lit doorway.

The hallway is lined with gilt framed paintings which appear out of focus in the background.

The table servers are tall, with straight military-like postures, wearing extravagantly decorated white uniforms. The table servers are carrying glistening, oversized, brilliant golden domed food trays.

Off in the distance, shrill delighted laughter grows louder, accompanying the delicate clinking of wine glasses.

The sound of hunting horn thrills add to the air of happy celebration.

The table servers enter the banquet hall from the far end, the servants' entrance, walking toward the huge, ornate banquet table in the foreground.

Gilt frame photos adorn the walls in the background while a full wall video flickers on another wall.

Tall, sleek candles burning in bright golden holders, along-side shiny gold cutlery tastefully decorate the fine linen table cloth.

Sparkling gilded wine glasses gently touch with echoes of "Cheers!". The shrill, delighted laughter of voices grows ever louder.

For all the lively sounds reverberating far beyond the banquet room, only three people are sitting at the table.

Two younger women and one older woman who is old enough to be their mother toast each other. They are all dressed in high fashion, diner party evening gowns.

The younger women are laughing in exaggerated, almost hysterically thrilled tones as if they were happily drunk and giddy. They are.

Each woman widens her eyes, squeals with delight and applauds enthusiastically as the table servers arrive and flash open the golden domed trays in rapid succession, in front of the three women, revealing trays of very large, wonderfully garnished dishes featuring entire pheasants, fish, etc. followed by trays filled with delicate, decorative, and generous portions of deserts.

Long after the table servers withdraw, leaving the women to eat without supervision, a new procession appears in the long corridor leading to the banquet hall.

From the starting point of the corridor, only the backs of three figures can be seen as they walk unceremoniously down the candlelit hallway toward the brightly lit doorway of the banquet hall.

Unlike the table servers before them, these figures are carrying only bulky, shiny aluminum metal valises.

The uniforms of these figures have the word "Forensics" inscribed on their backs. These are scientists.

The forensic scientists enter the banquet hall. Police are milling about. The one in charge greets the arriving trio, saying, "Table for three?"

He's Jim, a greying veteran of the police force who's known for his dry sense of humour.

Cathy, supervisor of the forensic scientists replies, "What's on the menu tonight?" It's 4 a.m.

Always quick, Jim replies, "You name it, we've got it. It's a gourmet feast that's fit for those three superbly-dressed victims. They each come with a side order of no witnesses. Bon appetit."

"It looks too fancy for a cafeteria. No table servers?" Cathy responds.

"Not one." Jim says.

"Economy measure?" Cathy quips.

"I doubt it. Not this party. It's not an all-you-can-eat bargain buffet. The booze alone probably cost enough to pay for my retirement pension." Jim says.

Cathy smirks, "Retirement? You don't even take vacations. How long has it been, ten years?"

"Tell me about it. This wingding set somebody back a load of cash." Jim says.

Carefully approaching the banquet table, Cathy and her team survey their crime scene and begin making photographic and mental notes.

The three women seated at the table are now bent over to the waist. Their heads face down, foreheads on the table.

David from the coroner's office is crouching behind one of the women at the table, studying the cadavers intently.

Cathy steps up to the table beside David, slowly and carefully turning her head until it's almost parallel with the woman in front of David.

Cathy's face takes on a puzzled look as she sees a substantial pile of very large coins in front of the woman directly in front of David and Cathy.

"Big tipper. Were these coins in front of her when you got here, David?" Cathy says.

"Yes. They look like yellow and white gold." David replies.

Cathy uses her forensic tweezers to pick up one small white fragment in the pile of coins.

"Is this what I think it is?" Cathy says.

"It's part of a chipped tooth. There are lots of them here." David gestures toward other tooth fragments on the table.

"Could you lift her shoulders so we can have a look at her face?" Cathy says.

"Sure." David says, as he attempts to lift the body. But the body doesn't move. "I'm sorry, I can't do it. She looks light, but she's too heavy for me."

Cathy smiles as if David were joking about his strength. She sees him flip much bigger dead weight cadavers than this one.

"Let's try together, on the count of three. One – two--three! Oh! She is heavy for her size!" Cathy says as she almost loses her balance after she and David fail to budge the body.

But there is movement and a jingling of tumbling coins.

As David and Cathy manage to raise the woman's neck her mouth opens wide and the table in front of her is suddenly inundated with a great flow of coins spilling out of her open mouth, quickly forming a huge pile under her raised chin and spilling across the table in front of her.

A candle is falling and there is no sign that the flow of coins is going to stop.

Cathy shouts, "Stop! Put her down!" Wondering if it can be done at all Cathy shouts again, "Gently!"

Too late. The head lands with a great thud and the avalanche of coins go flying in every direction.

The body almost slips from their grip. Two more candles topple.

"Sorry Cathy!" Young David is embarrassed and in pain. He bends over in apparent agony with his hand behind his back.

Cathy crouches over David's bent figure, "It's your back again?" Turning to an officer standing a distance away, Cathy says, "Give him a hand, Mike."

Mike helps David move away from the table.

While David struggles with his pain, Cathy leans over and focuses on the coins sparkling across banquet table.

"Whatever happened to the cashless society?" Cathy asks herself out loud. "Nick, could you bring me the optic fiber camera?"

Forensic scientist Nick gingerly slides the slim camera tube over the coins on the table, into the dead woman's gaping open mouth, down her throat, and along her oesophagus.

They're all sparkling inside with coins.

With considerable care and difficulty, the three forensic scientists and their police helpers manage to put the bodies into body bags and help the body wagon crew load the bags into the back of their vehicle.

It takes much longer than it normally would for the wagon to cover the ten kilometres from the location of the banquet hall to the crime lab.

Much later, with the help of two assistants, The coroner places a very large, transparent plastic bag full of shiny, bloody coins beside five other full bags of the same, already on the side of an examination table.

Cathy enters the room and greets the coroner with a question, "Death by overeating?"

Always ready to educate, the coroner replies in a professorial serious tone, "Did you know that obesity is now considered a pandemic? It's an extremely expensive problem too.

"The health system is spending about a hundred billion dollars every year on obesity-related illness. And that's only in this country."

Pointing at the bodies of his autopsy report, the coroner continues, "These three diners spent their last night alive trying to initiate themselves into the problem.

"But this doesn't appear to be their usual eating pattern. They were new at gorging themselves, just getting started.

"None of them show any indication of habitually overeating.

"Their fat levels aren't anywhere near excessive. They're definitely not obese." the coroner concludes.

"So this probably isn't heart failure due to long-term self-abuse and a massive cholesterol buildup?" Cathy says.

"No, this is binge eating. Their stomach contents are like a smorgasbord, consisting of various types of birds, fish, and several cuts of pork and beef, not to mention several varieties of vegetables, fruit, and pastry." the coroner says.

"They literally stuffed themselves to death. In only one meal, these three women consumed enough food for a family of twelve, for an entire week.

"But the food itself doesn't appear to be the cause of death." the coroner says.

"They weren't poisoned?" Cathy wonders out loud.

"I found no obvious signs of poisoning, Cathy. The COD is clearly asphyxiation for two of your diners.

"The other died just short of asphyxiation. Her COD is a broken neck, due the weight of the coins in her mouth and oesophagus."

Entering the autopsy room and hearing the coroner's last words, David holds his back with his left hand and winces, wondering if he has to decide which is worse, his back pain or the mishap at the crime scene.

"Did I break her neck?" David gasps out in anxious tones.

The coroner replies in a soothing, reassuring tone, "No, David. It was broken by the coins long before you arrived at the scene."

"All three victims consumed so much food and money, in such a short period of time that they didn't have any space left over for eating or breathing.

"Their stomachs and digestive organs are completely saturated with a mixture of food, coins, and paper money."

The coroner holds up flat, thin lungs to emphasize his point.

"The oesophagus became so full and heavy that it made breathing impossible and actually flattened the lungs."

"It sounds as if the victims had a combination of bulimia and pica." Cathy interjects.

"You're thinking this banquet was a last supper for three people suffering from the same eating disorders?" the coroner says.

"Is that possible?" Cathy says.

"You'll have to tell me the answer to that one, Cathy. Judging from the money diet, you could be right about the pica.

"But none of the victims shows any signs of the conditions usually associated with pica.

"I think we can probably rule out bulimia too, because the victims made sure they would become physically incapable of vomiting.

"Their internal muscles were incapacitated, too weighted down by the coins to push out food.

The victims were too chocked up to either vomit or call for help. In each victim, the larynx and trachea were too badly crushed to function normally." the coroner says.

"Is there any evidence they were force fed?" Cathy says.

The coroner uses a metal pry to open one victim's mouth wider, revealing the interior, exposing the tongue and throat. There are no tonsils.

"All the tearing around the lips seems to point to forced feeding.

"The lips are badly cut and bruised. The inner mouth is filled with lacerations. Notice that the rough edges of the coins actually cut off her tonsils." the coroner says.

"The pain would be excruciating without anaesthesia." the coroner says.

"They were probably using alcohol as a pain killer. That's why we found so many empty wine bottles in the banquet hall." Cathy adds.

The coroner picks up a dental tool and exposes the remains of teeth and gums.

There are bits of chipped, cracked, broken teeth in the mouth, and small jagged edges of roots still inside the gums, which are torn and ripped.

"They'd need lots of pain killer. There's chipping every-where and some nasty abrasions along the gum line. There's almost nothing left of the teeth." the coroner says.

"It's worse than any bar fight homicides I've ever seen." Cathy says.

"Yet there are no signs of external blunt force trauma of any kind." the coroner says.

"Cathy, did you know that I almost switched to dentistry when I was in med school? Fortunately, I changed my mind."

"You didn't want to spend the rest of your life looking at bad teeth and inhaling bad breath?" Cathy says.

"It wasn't that so much as the possibility of having to make extractions. Pulling teeth would have been like performing an autopsy on someone who was still alive." the coroner says.

"The tooth and gum damage you see here is typical of all three banquet victims.

"There are no signs that these injuries resulted from the actions of anyone but the victims themselves.

"No one else was prying open their mouths and shovelling in the food and money. The banquet victims were deliberately swallowing at the time of death." the coroner says.

"According to the stomach contents, early in the meal the food is very well-chewed. Later it wasn't. The deterioration of their teeth account for that difference.

"Striations in the oesophagus indicate voluntary swallowing directionality which is toward the stomach, not away from it.

"There is no evidence that any of the victims were trying to void anything already in their stomachs or any of the morsels heading that way.

"Each victim was evidently attempting to force-feed herself. She was pushing coins down her own throat. She was literally trying to stuff herself with money.

"I've never been that hungry." Cathy says. Pointing at small bags on side table, she adds, "These small bags look familiar."

"They're the same kind of sachets used by drug mules, small enough to swallow easily and to void at the other end." the coroner explains.

"They had drug bags in their bodies too?" Cathy says, intrigued.

"Yes Cathy, but these bags were full of money, not drugs.

"In addition to the large volume of coins inside the victims' bodies there were a considerable number of these little bags full of $1000 bills in their stomachs.

"In fact, the stomachs were so full of coins that some of the bags were sliced up and burst open, becoming a money paste on the lining of the stomach during digestion." the coroner says.

"Indigestion." Cathy says.

"There's something else." the coroner says, "A residue of some kind is present on both the coins and the bags.

"The residue isn't related to any naturally occurring bodily fluid. I suspect it's a lubricant.

"I also found another unidentified substance in the food itself, which I've also sent to tox for analysis.

"This substance is present in very large quantities in the undigested food." the coroner says.

"There's just one other thing that I find particularly strange." the coroner says, pointing at one of the bodies.

"Victim number two appears to have been suffering from self-induced malnutrition. She was anorexic." the coroner concludes.

"In the end she was dying to eat." Cathy says.

•••••

Lab technician Greg is looking at a fingerprint analyzing computer, trying to find matches for all the prints found at the banquet hall.

"What have you got?" Cathy says as she enters the lab.

"Nick sent us prints from nine different people so far." Greg says, "As you'd expect, the food trays are covered with prints from the food servers. And the prints of all five of them are in the system."

"Are you saying we already have five suspects?" Cathy says.

"Not exactly. The servers are in the system because they're all ex-military." Greg says.

"Food specialists?" Cathy says.

"Maybe they were carrying the food to serve and protect the money." Greg says. "This feast would need a security detail."
"Anything else?" Cathy says.

"There's still one unknown set of prints to run. Nick just sent them from the crime scene." Greg says. "I've already identified one of the victims and I'm running the other two."

The print lab computer screen flashes the words "positive match". The driver's license of one of the victims pops up on screen.

"Who are you?" Greg says.

DNA specialist Wendy enters the print lab, looks at the screen, and hands the DNA report to Cathy.

"Two of the victims are sister." Wendy says.

"I can see the family resemblance." Greg says, looking over Cathy's shoulder at the DNA results.

"What about the third victim?" Cathy says.

"Only one of the two sisters shares DNA with the other victim." Wendy says, pointing at the face on the computer screen.

"The third victim is her mother, but not her sister's mother.

·····

Nick and Ray are still at the banquet hall crime scene, examining the many large framed photographs on every wall.

They are pictures of scenes of starvation and famine around the world.

Nick removes each picture from the wall to look at the back of the frame.

On the back of each one is printed: "Property of FPMJ Foundation".

Ray finds a full wall video computer projector and begins playing a video that begins with "The FPMJ Foundation Presents."

Next on the video, a man walks in front of the camera and says:

"Hello. I'm Tyrone Stauners, vice-president of The FPMJ Foundation. The story you are about to see is true. This story is about the daily life experience of most people alive today.

"They make up more than 80 per cent of the world population. But they get less than a 20 per cent share of the world's food sup- ply and other resources.

"For the rest of us, life is exactly the opposite.

"Here in the industrialized world we have less than 20 per cent of the world population. But we're consuming more than 80 per cent of the world's food supply and other resources.

"We're taking a huge bite out of the world. We're eating too much. That's why we're becoming more and more obese and diabetic." Stauners says.

The video cuts to images of very obese people in the industrialized world who are stuffing themselves with super sized helpings of food and struggling to walk.

Stauners' voice-over continues to narrate: "We're taking far more than our fair share.

"We're taking the food out of other people's mouths.

"Every day, hundreds of millions of children are going hungry and starving to death because we're eating their share of the world's food supply." Stauners says.

The video shows starving children who look like no more than skin stretched over bones. The video cuts to a close up of Stauners.

"As Mahatma Gandhi once said, 'Live simply so that others can simply live.' Otherwise, we're giving the rest of the world only two choices, revolution or death.

"If we don't act now, there could soon be a global uprising against the industrialized world. That's us. Hyper-inflation in food prices is already causing rioting in some countries..."

Ray ejects the video, puts it inside an evidence bag, seals and signs it.

"I don't get it, Ray." Nick says, "I'm losing my appetite every time I look at these walls. How could the three victims eat anything?

"Why didn't they feel sick to their stomachs? If you're going to gorge yourself with food, why do in it in a room full of pictures of people going hungry?" Nick says.

"I agree that it's in very bad taste, Nick. But I also know how this foundation operates.

"A few years ago, one of my former colleagues at the university was a member of the board at the FPMJ Foundation.

"It's a legitimate NGO with a very aggressive approach to fundraising. Apparently, their educational and foreign aid projects are helping to make the world a better place." Ray explains.

"Do you think our crime scene was some kind of educational project that got out of hand?" Nick says.

"I hope not, Nick. But the FPMJ Foundation does belong to the Stauners family. They have a reputation for doing whatever it takes to get what they want."

Nick hears his phone and sees Greg's name on screen. Then the text message comes up: "Unknown prints match found."

Nick turns to Ray, "It's from Greg." He says the unknown prints belong to Tyrone Stauners. Let's find out if he'd commit murder to get what his family wants."

Nick and Ray return to the forensics building. Tyrone Stauners is waiting for them. They all shake hands and go to an interview room.

Nick opens a folder and spreads photos of the banquet hall FPMJ Foundation pictures on the interview table.

"Thank you for coming to talk with us Mr. Stauners. I've heard a lot about your foundation." Ray says.

"All good, I'm sure. You were a bit vague on the phone. What exactly is this all about?" Stauners says.

"Do these pictures belong to your foundation, Mr. Stauners?" Nick asks.

"Why, yes they do." Stauners says after looking carefully.

"We use them to persuade people to make donations for our world hunger projects.

"Did you take these pictures at one of our fundraisers? They're protected by copyright, you know."

Ignoring the copyright remark, "Not exactly. They were at at a crime scene." Nick says.

"Crime scene? As far as I know, none of our pictures are missing. I haven't had any reports of a theft." Stauners says in an alarmed tone.

"Do you think someone stole these pictures from our foundation?"

"It's not a case of theft, Mr. Stauners. It's three dead people." Nick says, spreading crime scene photos of the victims on the table.

"Do you recognize any of these people?" Nick says.

"Of course. That's my Aunt Frances and these are my cousins Patsy and Mary-Joe. What happened to them?" Stauners says.

"We're not sure. I'm sorry for your loss." Nick says.

"Thanks. But, frankly, we weren't close, not at all." Stauners says unemotionally.

"When was the last time you saw them?" Nick says.

"We had to meet for some family business a few weeks ago." Stauners says.

"We found your fingerprints all over these pictures. Are you sure you didn't see your aunt and cousins last night, at the banquet hall?" Nick says.

"I've handled all of the foundation pictures. I have to approve each one before it can be put on display.

"I'd be very surprised if you didn't find my fingerprints on them." Saunders says, looking at his watch and beginning to stand and leave.

"I'm sorry I can't be of any further help to you, or to them. I really must go now. I have a board meeting to attend. We're going to approve a new project today."

Stauners is on his feet, looking toward the door, all the while looking worriedly at his watch.

He pauses briefly, picks up the photos of the victims, shakes his head slowly, sighs, and drops them casually in front of Ray.

•••••

Holdrige comes out of his lab and meets Cathy going the other way in the forensics building corridor.

"I have the tox reports from the coroner's samples." Holdrige says.

"And?" Cathy says, not wanting to get into one of Holdrige's prolonged small talk conversations with little content about the case."

"The residue on the coins is a derivative of sea algae, agar-agar. It's jello." Holdrige says.

"Flavor?" Cathy says.

"Neutral." Holdrige says without going off on a tangent.

"What's the other unknown substance?" Cathy says.

"Progestogens, specifically corficosteriod and megestrol acetate." Holdrige says.

"Appetite stimulants." Cathy says.

"That's probably why the victims couldn't resist eating until they died." Holdrige says.

"But why would anyone need appetite stimulants with all that delicious food on the table? And why eat the money? People spend money. They don't eat it." Cathy says, almost to herself.

This is Holdrige's cue to start the small talk.

"I think it was probably like a birthday party. You know, parents give their kids a birthday cake full of money wrapped in bits of wax paper.

"Is there any indication that this was a birthday party that went overboard?" Holdrige says.

"Not so far." Cathy says, making a concerted effort not to say anything sarcastic.

"But I know all about money in birthday cakes. When when my daughter was little she actually swallowed some coins in her cake.

"She had to take strong laxatives at the hospital. After that, she was very careful whenever she ate anything."

Quickly returning to topic, Cathy says, "The banquet victims were adults. They were swallowing gold coins and sachets of $1000 bills.

"So they were taking appetite stimulants to make the money palatable. Only the anorexic victim needed stimulants to eat so much food and keep it down.

"All of them obviously wanted to fill up on the bills and coins." Cathy says.

"An expensive family suicide pact?" Holdrige says.

"We'll see. Good work Holdrige." Cathy has to find Nick.

Holdrige beats her to it, walking away smiling, as Nick comes around the corner. Puzzled by Holdrige's smile, Nick smiles back in passing.

Holdrige turns and says, "Nick, I think Cathy wants to see you."

Cathy comes from the other direction, addressing only Nick, "What have you got, Nicky?"

"I'm not sure yet. Tyrone Stauners' prints are at the crime scene but they don't place him there.

"Only his foundation pictures and video are right in the middle of it. If the banquet wasn't a fundraising event, why were the pictures and video there?" Nick says.

"What do we know about the foundation?" Cathy says.

"It's a multi-million dollar operation, donating money and sending volunteers to places like Africa and Central America to help with locally-sponsored agricultural projects." Nick says.

"According to the annual report, the foundation saves millions of people from malnutrition and disease every year." Nick says.

"It's all run by the Tyrone Stauners?" Cathy says.

"No. He's just running things while his father Jeffrie Stauners is out of the country visiting projects. Jeffrie Stauners is the real head honcho." Nick says.

"Have you talked to Jeffrie Stauners?" Cathy says.

"He's out of the country visiting a project in Central America. He's in Costa Rica right now."

"Costa Rica? We should send someone to interview him." Cathy says, smiling.

"I know just the team for the job." Nick says, returning the smile with a knowing nod.

•••••

It's hot and humid in Costa Rica, as it always is between hurricane seasons.

A woman in an adobe hut sits with her back to the wall, leaning over a desk and poising a pen over a sheet of letter writing paper. She begins writing.

She's Sara, a forensic scientist who works with Cathy and her colleagues for seven years.

Sara writes:

"Dear Cathy, I've wanted to write to you for a long time, but I didn't know how to start.

"It's hard for me to express just how happy I am here in this para-dise. Gil and I are both getting a fresh start in life. It's easy here because this place is so full of life.

"We're connecting with so many amazing living things. They seem to be coming to life all around us, every day. They're flour-ishing instead of dying.

"It's a far cry from processing crime scenes..."

Sara closes her eyes and plays back the past two years.

She and Gil are standing outside together, looking at a beautiful scene of colourful tropical birds, animals, plants, and insects. Gil is concentrating on the insects.

Sara and Gil are pointing, taking pictures, and smiling at each other.

Continuing to write, Sara strokes the pen on paper:

"What a wonderful experience this is, after so many years of spending all our time with dead people, people who had their lives abruptly cut short for no good reason.

The rainy season doesn't bother me anymore. I used to get de-pressed.

"I guess I'm finally getting over my own near death experience in the desert, and how badly it made me feel for such a long time af-terwards. I hope...

Interrupting, Gil pokes his head through the door, "Sara?" He's waving a letter size piece of paper at Sara. She breaks into a warm smile.

"A courier brought this. It's Cathy. She needs our help."

"I'm ready. Let me see that."

Sara drops her pen on the desk and walks toward Gil, taking the paper out of his hand.

"Please call Cathy. And, could you come back into town with me now, Sara?" Sara is already reaching for the phone.

•••••

Miguel, a foreign aid worker enters a hut on the edge of the Costa Rican forest, approaching a man sitting at a desk. Letterhead on the desk reveals that this is a field camp of "FPMJ Foundation".

"Señor Stauners." the aid worker says, motioning in the direction of a man and women waiting outside the hut while a brilliant tropical sun accentuates their profiles. The man is wearing a large straw hat. "Dos estranjeiros."

"Gracias, Miguel." Jeffrie Stauners is swiftly at the door welcoming his visitors.

Jeffrie makes no effort to hide his excitement as if he's about to meet his favourite celebrities. He is.

"I can hardly contain myself. It's such a delight to meet both of you. Please come in! It's so sultry outside. I'm never here long enough to get adjusted to the climate.

Repeating himself, "It's such a pleasure to meet you both!

"Thanks for seeing us." Sara says.

"Oh, not at all." Jeffrie smiles.

"It's good to meet you, Mr. Stauners. I've read so much about your foundation's work to eliminate starvation and malnutrition in the world." Gil says.

Sara smiles, studying Stauners' face while he talks to Gil, looking for a baseline to use to determine his reactions to the questions that she and Gil are about to ask.

Sara never forgets her training.

Jeffrie can't stop laying on the praise.

"The work you two are doing in entomology and rare species is helping to keep the whole planet alive and protecting the environment that supports all life.

"We do need both food and a good place to live now, don't we?" Jeffrie says.

"Thanks, but we're only two members of a good team." Gil says, almost shrugging off the compliment. "We work with people from all over the world. They do most of the work."

"I'd say you're the star players." Jeffrie insists. "You certainly live up to your reputations for modesty.

"I know about your remarkable success in forensics too. So I'm especially glad to meet you today.

"It gives me the opportunity to, you know, come clean, as they say in police work. I have a confession to make."

Sara leans forward, looking for a sign that Jeffrie isn't joking. Gil looks sceptical, but intrigued.

"I've always been a big fan of forensic scientists." Jeffrie says.

"Thank you Mr. Stauners. Good forensics is professional team work at its best too." Gil says.

"I've always wondered why you both retired from forensic work?" Jeffrie says.

"It's complicated. Maybe we can talk about that another time." Sara interjects.

"Oh, I don't mean to pry. Forensic's lose is the world's gain." Jeffrie says apologetically.

"You're bringing the same determination and driving force to solving world problems that are pushing us here at The FPMJ Foundation.

"You inspire our people and encourage us all to try harder too. We want to help make the world a better place just as much as you do." Jeffrie says.

Gil reverts to the official tone he has not used since leaving the forensics team. He hasn't lost the knack for lack of practice.

"We appreciate your words, but we're not here to gather praise. We're here for evidence. We have a specific purpose for being here.
"We're trying to help our former colleagues in forensics science to solve a case involving your foundation. They asked us to talk to you.

"Of course we have no official status in the investigation, and you are under no obligation to talk to us. Your cooperation is entirely voluntary but we'd appreciate it." Gil says.

"Oh, you want to interrogate me for a case. Bravo! I'm looking forward to that." Jeffrie bubbles with enthusiasm. "This is my first case!"

"Don't worry about the jurisdictional formalities. I'd be glad to help in any way that I can. Go right ahead.

"Please ask whatever questions you wish and I'll do my best to provide answers."

Calming down a bit, Jeffrie adds "What are they investigating?" He has a serious countenance and earnest expression for the first time.

Sara takes a mental note of Stauner's facial muscles as a reference point and says, "They're looking into the death of three members of your family. We're sorry for your loss."

"Oh! Dreadful business! They died as they lived." Jeffrie says in subdued tones.

Quickly Gil adds, "So you've already received the news about your sister-in-law and nieces?"

"Yes. Actually, she was my late brother-in-law's second wife. Frances. Technically, she's almost not a relative at all, not a blood relative.

"Frances was Patsy's mother. Mary-Joe was Frances' step daughter, from my brother-in-law's first marriage.

"My son Tyrone called and told me about their death this morning. It was a terrible shock, but not completely unexpected. I guess it was inevitable." Jeffrie says, shrugging.

"Why's that?" Sara says with the precision of a direct hit. She's good at cutting to the chase.

Jeffrie looks uncomfortable as he says,"I knew they'd kill themselves eventually. It was just a matter of time.

"Those three women were completely self-absorbed and self-destructive, the antithesis of The FPMJ Foundation.

"What absolute irony! Did you know that the foundation is named after them? It's the Frances-Patsy-Mary-Joe Foundation." Jeffrie says.

"They used to be such generous, loving people, but they changed for the worst a few years ago. It wasn't a happy time after my brother-in-law Joe remarried."

"How did they change?" Gil asks.

Sounding evasive for the first time, Jeffrie says, "Joe didn't change at all, but those three women began trying to com-pensate for their unhappiness by spending lavish amounts of money.

"They became increasingly wasteful and extravagant. It was appalling.

"They stopped thinking about the implications of their way of life. They completely ignored the wider world around them." Jeffrie says.

"I just don't understand. What was wrong with them?" Jeffrie seems to be talking to himself.

"For me, those women became like a metaphor and a microcosm of our present world order.

"In today's world, less than 20 per cent of we humans can indulge ourselves almost without limits.

"We can have anything we want. We can eat as much as we desire. But this dream world is really a nightmare for us." Jeffrie looks sad.

"More and more of us are obese. We have diabetes, heart problems, cancers, and endless neuroses, aches, and pains that aren't natural. We acquire them.

"We have maladies that were almost unknown to our grandparents." Jeffrie says.

"We have drawers full of every imaginable type of high-priced prescription drug which claims to cure us.

"The opulence depresses us too. Material wealth is not enriching our lives at all.

"We've become addicted to pain killers." Jeffrie says.

"None of the drugs really do anything to help us. They don't really cure our basic illness – extreme self-indulgence.

"Our dream world is also a nightmare for the rest of our human family." Jeffrie pauses, looking out the door into the sunlight branches of palm trees.

"While we mindlessly indulge ourselves, more than 80 per cent of we humans are struggling every day just to get by."

"All they get is the bare essentials of life." Jeffrie gazes off in the distance again, looking almost hopeless.

Looking at Gil and Sara, Jeffrie continues, "Sorry, it really gets to me. I know you've seen it too."

"Yes, we have. Please go on." Sara says with visible and sincere sympathy.

"People are walking too many kilometres on empty stomachs every day, starting very early in the morning, only so that they can stand in long lineups just to collect enough drops of water to survive for a day.

"The first thing that we do every day is to urinate into potable water." Jeffrie says as Sara nods slowly in agreement.

"People are working very hard to scrape together just enough food to keep themselves and their children alive one more day." Jeffrie continues.

"What's wrong with us? What kind of people are we? We're in the middle of the biggest crime scene in the world.

"It's the one that my foundation is trying to find solutions to all the time." Jeffrie says, taking a deep breath before continuing.

"I'm sorry to interrupt you Mr. Stauners. I know that we need to find those solutions if we're going to survive as a species." Gil says with sincerity and conviction.

"Sara and I would be glad to talk to you about solving the crime you're talking about any time, but our objective here today is much more modest.

"Our former colleagues in forensic science are trying to find out why your nieces and brother-in-law's wife didn't survive." Gil says.

Jeffrie, sounding a bit frustrated, says, "That's what I'm trying to tell you. Those people were killing themselves for years. They obviously didn't want to survive."

"Yet their behaviour says exactly the opposite too." Gil says. "Are you familiar with fruit flies, Mr. Stauners?"

Bewildered by the change of subject to a minor insect, Jeffrie says with impatience, "Only as an annoyance."

"Fruit flies live an entire lifetime in less than two months. During that short time, they seem to hover around aimlessly, devouring everything they can."

With visible annoyance Stauners says, "You're point!?"

"Fruit flies pass their whole lives that way. They don't change their behaviour." Gil continues.

"And after less than two months, they die because it is in their nature, not because they hovered and devoured."

"I'm sorry, sir." Jeffrie says apologetically, regaining his composure and asking Gil in a more formal and respectful tone, "I'm not an entomologist like you, sir. I don't quite follow you."

Intervening to simplify Gil's familiar tact of using insect metaphors, Sara says, "Okay. Let's put it this way – You say your nieces and your brother-in-law's wife lived extravagantly.

"Their big, flashy banquet is evidence that you're right.

"You also say they were trying to make up for their unhappy family life by spending lots of money. They were gobbling up as much as they could, like fruit flies." looking at Gil.

Looking back at Jeffrie again, "So, why would they suddenly give it all up?

"Why would they deliberately end their lives, instead of trying to prolong their lives and grab more wealth? It doesn't make any sense." Sara says.

Jeffrie grapples with Sara's explanation and questions, "I see. You think that, maybe, they were murdered.

"But..." Jeffrie looks to Gil for support, "Unfortunately, the only resemblance they had to fruit flies was that they were living as if there were no tomorrow."

"They were selfish wretches. If I were comparing them with insects, I'd compare them with locusts." Jeffrie looks directly at Gil again.

"They couldn't stop themselves. So no one would have to push them very hard to get them to kill themselves. It was in their self-destructive nature." Jeffrie says.

"If you're looking for a murderer, you may as well look for a fruit fly's ghost. Let me show you something."

Jeffrie abruptly pulls away from his lounge chair, walks toward his desk, and removes a document from one of the drawers.

Sara almost instinctively reaches for a holster that she hasn't worn for two years. It's a reflex reaction.

She catches herself having a slight relapse of the post-traumatic stress which haunts her for months after she retires from forensic work. She's all right. She recomposes herself.

·····

Back in the forensics building, Cathy's administrative boss Conrad catches her in the hallway, leaving the quiet room where everyone has to take a break every day to maintain their sanity.

Conrad motions Cathy aside, to a more secluded spot on the edge of the hallway. He speaks softly but assertively.

"I just had a meeting with the District Attorney." Conrad says.

"We can't officially use Gil and Sara in this investigation. They don't work here any more. If they collect any evi-dence free lance, we might not be able to use it in court."

"Anything they do in Central America is way out of our jurisdiction." Conrad says.

"The D.A. had a call from the State Department too.

"The FPMJ Foundation is well connected in D.C. There are all sorts of legal complications and political mine fields ahead of us." Conrad explains in cautious tones.

"Politics is your job, not ours." Cathy retorts, always perplexed by the political bureaucracy.

"We're just trying to do our job. Gil trained everyone in my team. Gil and Sara know their legal status.".

"Besides, the budget cuts don't give us any choice. You're always reminding us to watch our costs." Cathy says.

"We can't afford to send anyone overseas.

"You know that when Jim had your job he spent so many years worrying about our budget that he's stopped himself from taking a vacation for ten years." Sara reminds Conrad.

"We have to make the most of the free help that Gil and Sara are giving us. We need them." Cathy argues definitively.

In a clearly chastened tone, Conrad replies, "I know. I know. All I'm saying is that we can't make a case and get a conviction on the basis of their help, not even in this case."

"Don't worry." Cathy says. "We're collecting evidence right here in our jurisdiction. Our case will be based on our findings.

"Gil and Sara are just doing us a favour and helping point us in the right direction." Cathy says.

•••••

Greg and Riley are arriving at the offices of "International Catering". A woman approaches them.

"I'm Greg and this is Riley from the crime lab. Are you the manager?"

"Yes. I'm Heather. What can I do for you?"

Greg takes some general photos of the crime scene out of his valise and shows them to Heather and asks her, "Did your company cater this event?"

Heather puts on her reading glasses and quickly peruses the photos.

"Yes we did." Heather says matter-of-factly. "We've had no complaints. Why do you ask? Is there some problem with the client?"

Greg replies, "There were no table servers in the banquet hall when we arrived. Can you explain why they left the scene of a crime without calling 9-1-1."

"Immigration status? I have no idea. They don't work for me. We only provided the food. The table servers were from a security company.

"They gave us nothing but trouble. You'd think they were with the Secret Service." Heather says with frustration.

"They were looking over my chefs' shoulders all the time when they were preparing the meals.

"When everything was ready for delivery to the table, those people searched everyone in the kitchen.

"Those so-called table servers were even scanning our chefs and trying to frisk them." Heather says.

"They almost caused a walkout by harassing our chefs, trying to tell them how to do their jobs. I was on the phone for a long time, calming down the chefs.

"Look, if those guys did something wrong it doesn't surprise me. They're not interested in providing clients with good service."

Greg interrupts Heather, "They were bothering your chefs because of the money, weren't they?"

"That's right. I've never heard of anything like it." Heather says. "My assistant tells me those guys put more money into the meal than the clients paid us for the catering job."

Riley asks, "Whose idea was it to add the appetite stimulants?"

Surprised, Heather says, "We don't do that sort of thing.

"First of all, our cuisine is superb. No one would ever require any sort of appetite stimulant to eat what we prepare in our kitchens.

Heather takes a tray off her desk and offers some scrumptious hors d'oeuvres to Riley and Gregg. They eat and smile.

Riley to Gregg, "Nick would love this one." Greg nods and smiles.
"See what I mean." Heather says. If there was any tampering with the food, it must have been the security company.

"As I said before, they delivered the food to the banquet hall, not us."

Riley asks, "Can you tell us the name of the security company?"

"I have the business card." Heather motions, "Please wait here."

Greg and Riley leave the catering company building with the "World Security Company" business card in hand.

A quick phone call later and they're on their way to see a Mr. Rollands.

As they arrive at the security company and park their forensics truck, a man getting out of a car waves at them.

"Mr. Rollands?" Greg says.

"That's me. You must be from the crime lab. I'm having a busy night. Just tell me what you want?" Rollands says.

"We know you've been busy." Riley says, showing Rollands some crime scene photos.

"Looks bad." Rollands says, clearly surprised.

"Look. All we did was take care of a security check of the caterer's kitchen staff and then product delivery at the banquet hall.

"After we made the delivery, our job was done." Rollands says.

"Then you left." Greg says.

"Then my people left. That's what the clients wanted. After we put the food and funds on the table, they were on their own, self-service." Rollands says.

"When did you add the appetite stimulant to the food?" Riley says.
"We had no instructions to do that." Rollands says.

"We need a list of all of your people who worked on this banquet." Greg says.

"Okay. You got it." Rollands says, taking out his phone to make it happen. Someone from his staff brings out a list of employees with their addresses and phone numbers.

Back at forensic headquarters Cathy is in her office looking at photos of the banquet hall and the pictures on the walls there.

She picks up a dry cracker from a small plate on the side of her desk, looks at it unenthusiastically, and puts it down without taking a bite. Her phone rings. It's Gil.

"Gil! What did Jeffrie Stauners have to say?" Cathy says.

"He had mixed feelings about your banquet victims. He showed us a document you should see.

"I'm scanning and sending it to you now." Gil says, pushing the button on his computer to send the documents.

"Thanks Gil. Love to Sara." Cathy hangs up. A moment later the documents start appearing on her computer screen. Five minutes later she's calling Jim.

"You rang?" Jim says as he answers his phone and walks in through Cathy's office door at the same moment, smiling about the good timing.

"Gil and Sara have something for us." Cathy says.

"I hope it's not another jar of those grasshoppers. They get stuck between my teeth." Jim smiles again.

"It's much tastier. Have a look at this. We need to talk to Tyrone Stauners again."

•••••

A few hours later they're sitting in the interview room again with Tyrone Stauners.

Jim puts a copy of the document from Gil and Sara on the interview table, opens the pages to one that's dog-eared, and slides it across the table toward Stauners.

"Nobody's at the banquet table now, so you get to finish everything that's left." Jim says to Stauners.

"Sorry. Too cryptic. I don't understand." Stauners says.

"According to your uncle's Will, now that your aunt and cousins are out of the way, you're about to inherit quite a lot of money." Jim says.

"You're the only surviving heir to your uncle's fortune now. We call that motive."

"You haven't read the Will correctly. Most of the money will go to The FPMJ Foundation, not to me personally. I'm simply the benefactor of my family members' greed and excesses." Stauners says.

"You can save that line for the tax collectors. The Will has no strings attached." Jim says.

"There's nothing here saying how you have to spend the inheritance. And with your father out of the country most of the time, you pretty well have a carte blanche.

"You can spend all the money any way you want. Who's going to know?" Jim smirks.

"That's true, but I'm not like my aunt and cousins. My life is about doing good things for other people, not just myself." Stauners says defensively.

"What do you think I'm going to do, embezzle money? I'm very dedicated to The Foundation."

"Mr. Stauners, we obtained a warrant to search your accountant's office. He was very cooperative." Jim says.

"So we now have evidence implicating you in the deaths of your aunt and two cousins."

"We found invoices addressed to your foundation from a food processing plant specializing in applying gelatin coatings." Jim says, sliding some papers across the table.

"We also found a receipt from a pharmaceutical company showing your foundation ordered the same appetite stimulants found in the food eaten by your aunt and cousins.

"We also have a sworn statement from the manager of the catering company saying that its chefs placed gelatin coated coins and small bags of paper money inside the meals delivered to the banquet for your aunt and cousins.

"We have records from the Mint showing that your foundation recently ordered delivery of an unusually large quantity of gold coins. They're the same ones that were inside the food at the banquet."

Cathy slides more papers across the table to Stauners, studying his reaction as he reads them.

"This makes you our number one suspect in the deaths of your aunt and cousins. If you talk now we can charge you with assisted suicide instead of murder." Jim says.

"We know you doped the food to make it easier for your aunt and cousins to gorge themselves to death.

"You injected a lot of appetite stimulant to make it impossible for them to stop eating. You wanted to make sure they'd eat themselves to death?" Jim says.

"So you end up with the best spot in the banquet hall, everything's on the house, and your sitting at a table for one. Bon Appetite!" Jim concludes.

"If you've read my late uncle's Will carefully," Stauners counters, "you will know that The Foundation is named as the executor of the Will.

"So everything, including these receipts, are in The Foundation's name.

"Besides, I told you. I gain nothing from the deaths of my aunt and cousins. I also gain nothing from helping them eat as much as possible.

"The more they eat, the less The Foundation gets from my uncle's estate." Stauners says.

Cathy's phone rings and she looks at the screen. "Excuse us for a moment, Mr. Stauners. We have another visitor. Please wait here."

Jeffrie Stauners is already waiting in another interview room when Cathy and Jim arrive. Jeffrie begins talking as soon as they sit down.

"I owe you all an apology. I wasn't completely candid with your former colleagues in Costa Rica. I haven't revealed everything that I know about this case.

"I decided to tell you the rest of the story when I finally realized you would start considering my son Tyrone a murder suspect.

"Then I needed time to get here to avoid any further problems for my son. I love my family." Jeffrie says.

"Mr. Stauners, you must know that withholding evidence in a homicide investigation is a very serious matter. You can go to jail for that alone." Cathy warns.

"Of course. But there is no homicide." Jeffrie says.

"And, please correct me if I'm wrong, but I believe that your former colleagues in Costa Rica retired a few years ago

"They have no official status whatsoever in this crime investigation."

Jeffrie drinks some water from his glass on the table, then continues.

"I did seek the legal opinion of the Foundation's attorney before coming here.

"I am here voluntarily and I convinced our attorney that I would not require her services to speak with you. Was I mistaken?" Jeffrie raises an eyebrow and turns his head.

More interested in solving the case than pursuing Stauners for other reasons, Cathy asks for more information.

"Please tell us about the missing evidence you've bringing to our attention, Mr. Stauners."

"Well, you see, my brother-in-law's Will has a caveat that was not included in the version of the Will that I provided in Costa Rica.

"Of course I trust your former colleagues, but my job is to protect my family foundation. I knew that any tragic news about my family would cause a media frenzy.

"Every detail of the Will could end up on You Tube or in some popular scandal magazine TV show." Jeffrie says.

"To make sure that doesn't happen, I've brought you the caveat and you are welcome to look at it.

"But this document must not leave this room. I think it will clear up this case once and for all. There was no murder at the banquet hall." Jeffrie says.

•••••

It's nearly dawn by the time the forensic team has there wrap-up meeting before going home for a good day's sleep.

Cathy, Ray, Nick, and Greg are the first to arrive at the conference room table, drinking assorted beverages.

Cathy picks up a dry cracker and puts it down without opening her mouth, laughing instead and saying, "I may never eat again. This case is killing my appetite."

"Maybe we bit off more than we could chew this time. The victims and the murderers seem to be the same people." Greg replies. Ray interjects, "And a dead man solved the case. The uncle's Will sliced up his estate quite nicely.

"One big helping went to the FPMJ Foundation; quite a sufficient portion was for Tyrone; and another generous serving was dished out to the late wife and daughters.

"It would have kept them all in gravy for the rest of their lives."

"But the wife and daughters couldn't get enough." Nick says. "They wanted seconds. They were craving for even more.

"The caveat promised to serve up more money on a platter for them alone. All they had to do was order it and eat everything they could.

"They had a craving for that all-you-can-eat menu. So they decided to go for an extra piece of the pie." Nick says.

Greg adds, "They could have had as much as they wanted. But their eyes were much bigger than their stomachs."

Ray says, "It was a tempting morsel of money that they couldn't resist.

"So they used the caveat to get the uncle's estate to pick up the tab for their banquet, including the check from the caterer, the bill for gelatin coating, the extra charge for appetite stimulants, and the big tip for the security table servers."

"The caterer and the security company didn't know the appetite stimulants were already mixed into the ingredients for sauces and oils at the food processing plant, before they were delivered to the catering kitchen." Ray says.

Cathy speaks again, reviewing the evidence. "Only the wife and daughters knew those secret ingredients and the complete recipe for all the dishes on the table.

"They blended everything together and added more than a generous dash of stimulants.

"Then they set the security people at maximum heat to bring the chefs to a steady boil.

"Unfortunately for the three diners' planning, they miscalculated the quantities and their diner party was a flop on the table." Cathy says.

Greg continues, "Nobody died of food poisoning. It wasn't a murder. Nobody wanted these women to die. It wasn't a deliberate suicide or an assisted suicide.

"They had no intention of dying. They were only throwing a banquet to help themselves to the foundation's money.

"But the victims did die at their own hands, and mouths. They forked and spooned themselves to death." Greg says.

Nick says, "Jeffrie and Tyrone Stauners weren't accomplices, not before or after the fact. They were left off the guest list.

"They didn't know exactly what was on the menu.

"All the caveat told them to do was provide the banquet hall, decorate it with the fundraising pictures and video, and pay all the bills."

"Jeffrie and Tyrone Stauners only knew the details of the Will and its caveat because they were at the reading of the Will." Nick says.

Greg speaks again, "When the banquet was finally over, the Stauners' foundation got stuck with the check for arranging the meal.

"But that was a small price to pay to feast on everything, not just the leftovers." Greg says.

Ray adds, "Jeffrie and Tyrone Stauners knew the wife and daughters well enough to suspect they would do everything possible to make sure they could eat up a big chunk of the foundation's money, or die in the attempt.

"The wife and daughters were under no obligation to tell them everything about their plans.

"They had nothing to gain by revealing their plans to make it easier for them to eat more of the foundation money. Their greedy scheme was their ultimate undoing." Ray says.

Nick says, "They cooked their own gooses. By not revealing all their plans to anyone, they almost guaranteed that nobody would be able to save them from themselves.

"You might say they got their just desserts too. They were trying to take food out of the mouths of hungry people but ended up cutting themselves out of the Will." Nick says.

"Their banquet turned out to be the most successful fundraising event in the entire history of the foundation." Ray says.

"Their greed accomplished the exact opposite of what they wanted. The foundation gets to keep their share of the money.

"So it can help feed many more people for a long time." Ray says.

Cathy wraps up, "And in the end, nobody in this case was committing a crime. No laws were broken by anyone.

"So no charges are being laid and the D.A. is definitely not interested in prosecuting either the Stauners, their foundation, or anyone else.

"Conrad was told that this case is closed. He agrees there was no murder and the foundation is doing a lot of good things in the world. Politics!"

Greg adds, "Jeffrie Stauners told Gil and Sara that solving this case would be like looking for the ghost of a fruit fly. He was right.

"There was a murderer and he's a ghost. It's Jeffrie Stauner's brother-in-law Joe."

"Joe knew that the caveat to his Will could have two results. Either it would shock his wife and daughters into becoming better people, or it would cause their deaths.

"They had to choose between helping themselves to the money and helping people who don't get enough to eat.

"Unfortunately, the idea of stuffing themselves instead of helping others didn't turn their stomachs." Greg says.

Cathy speaks again, "So this time we couldn't speak for the dead. They'd already spoken to Joe's ghost before we got to the crime scene.

"The victims said they chose to die, even though they actually wanted to live."

At this moment Holdrige arrives in the conference room, hesitantly poking his head through the door.

Seeing smiles around the table, he ventures in, smiling himself and holding up a very large box.

"This just came from Luxury Catering. It's addressed to all of us. It's marked perishable.

Nick says, "More of that delectable evidence that Greg and Riley were collecting?"

Holdrige takes on his serious lab rat look. "I took the liberty of taking some samples and running a check on the ingredients. They're harmless.

"This appears to be breakfast.... Uh... I'll take this to the break room. Riley and Wendy are waiting for us there. Has anyone seen Jim?

Cathy says, "Do you really want to know?"

•••••

It's dawn in Costa Rica and Sara is looking at a silhouette of a man at the doorway to her abode. "Is that you Gil?"

"I'm over here, Sara." Gil says.

Sara to the man who's silhouette is still in her doorway, "Who are you?"

The silhouette figure is wearing an all white, casual suit. He's holding a bottle in one hand and a glass in the other. It's Jim.

Jim moves forward until his face become visible. He's smiling.

"Do you really want to know?"

A few moments later Jim, Sara, and Gil are sitting together at a table talking quietly.

"Ahhh. This is like old times." Jim says.

"Now come on you two, admit it. I want a full confession.

"Despite all the rough times and bad feelings before you left, you really miss the action, don't you?

"I saw your report. You're still professionals. You haven't lost your touch." Jim says with teasing conviction.

Gil says, "I prefer our life now, Jim. Coming here was the right thing for us to do.

"Sure, maybe I do feel slightly nostalgic when I think about those long nights of work and how we helped the dead tell their stories.

"We helped people who could no longer help themselves. You can't ever completely forget it. And it's worth remembering."

"We need to listen so that we can help people in tragic circumstances." Gil says.

Sara nods, saying, "We're listening better here too. We can hear our own hearts for a change. There was almost no time for that back in the forensics unit.

"We can even sleep at night now too. We're not chasing around from one crime scene to the next."

We're getting something more here than those long nights could ever give us. We can finally live our own lives.

"We're putting life before death. That's why we came here." Sara says.

"Our work in forensics still haunts me sometimes. But I feel better about our life now because we're still helping.

"We're helping living, breathing things, instead of listening only to the dead and damaged all the time. We're helping the living speak here." Sara says.

Gil speaks again, "We can find more in our lives if we look carefully. We can discover what we missed. We can make things better for ourselves and for everyone around us.

Jim smiles broadly at hearing about his friends' happiness. "Okay. I take it all back. You're not missing anything here.

"I'd say you two really have the best of both worlds. Thanks for helping us out at the crime lab one more time."

Raising his glass, Jim says, "Here's looking at you kids. This place is rejuvenating!"

"And thanks for inviting me here. Did you know that this is my first vacation in ten years? Cheers!"

Jane Drake is struggling to keep her vintage Tesla Roadster on the road through a massive electric storm, ignoring the vehicle's visual warning system.

ALERT! GREAT DANGER! TORNADO STRIKES! PULL OVER! TAKE NEAREST EXIT NOW! A female voice cautions in rising tones of concern.

The voice of Jane's boss punctuates the computer screen, "SO YOU DAMNED WELL BETTER GET OFF THE ROAD DRAKE!"

Jane habitually ignores her boss. She writes off the storm as typical "new weather".

Scientists attribute it to continued irreversible climate change that's creating an increasingly unstable world climate.

"You didn't listen to the warnings forty years ago and now we're paying the price." Jane says to herself, criticizing her boss' generation.

Almost blinding heavy sheet lightning illuminates the long empty horizon, flashing on Jane's defiant, determined, sardonic face.

Deafening thunder crashes almost simultaneously. Clouds billow in the later stages of tornado formation.

Now glaring lightning projects a giant shadow of Jane's sharp silhouette through the car windows, flashing for an instant onto a wall alongside her vehicle.

The "GOVERNMENT LANE: ELECTRIC VEHICLES ONLY" runway is completely deserted due to the raging storm.

Bureaucracy doesn't like uncertainty and unpredictable processes or outcomes.

Automated roadway warning systems issue an extreme danger signal – "IMMINENT COLLISION! TORNADO IMPACT IN ONE MINUTE. -59 seconds -58 seconds -57 seconds -56 seconds..."

The countdown to disaster continues, interrupted only by more alerts:

"VEHICLE CHASSIS STRESS FACTOR:
BEYOND CAPACITY.

VEHICLE DAMAGE ESTIMATE:
IRREPARABLE.

RECOMMENDED ACTION:
RECYCLING OF COMPONENTS.

DRIVER INJURY PROJECTION:
TOTAL DISMEMBERMENT.

EVASIVE ACTION RECOMMENDED:
UNAVAILABLE.

DIAGNOSTIC:
VEHICLE SAFETY PROTOCOLS
ARE NOT ENGAGED.

FOR FURTHER INFORMATION:
PLEASE CONSULT YOUR NEAREST
ELECTROCAR SERVICE CENTRE."

Jane Drake laughs and accelerates, turning off the annoying panicky system.

"This is a registered antique Tesla Roadster not one of those exploding and burning cars of the ancient petroleum age!" Jane shouts back at the suddenly blank screens at roadside.

Jane's Tesla Roadster flashes like a bullet toward a blank horizon past more government electronic signage, across empty, seemingly endless road.

She races on and on, never losing control or spinning out. In an instant she makes a very sharp abrupt turn.

"DESCEND NOW!" Jane shouts toward her on board computer.

A hidden road just as suddenly opens in front of her and below.

Jane's vehicle descends and the hidden entrance to a road closes behind her, just as a Level 5 tornado hits directly behind the vehicle's path, obliterating everything but its funnel cloud from view.

Jane accelerates again in the long tunnel, flashing past bright holographic illustrations reading Destination One.

It's only a momentary vanishing blur before a new message appears:

"EXTREME TUNNEL WARNING:
DECREASE VELOCITY! DECREASE VELOCITY! YOU
ARE IN VIOLATION OF
OFFICIAL SECURITY PROTOCOLS!
DECREASE VELOCITY IMMEDIATELY!"

Jane laughs again, accelerating more as she descends far-ther into the seemingly endless long tunnel.

"EXTREME VEHICLE WARNING:
SECURITY OVERRIDE ACTIVATED.

AUTOMATIC DECELERATION MODE ACTIVATED! PRE-
PARE FOR IMPACT!"

Jane is abruptly ejected and jettisoned forward through an opening suddenly appearing on the driver's side of her windshield.

Flying at G2 force, face distorted, she is involuntarily and gradually decelerating into very soft, protective white-balloons-like
plasma barrier.

A moment later Jane is released from "balloons".

"EMERGENCY SECURITY SCAN COMPLETE. PLEASE
PROCEED AGENT DRAKE."

The Tesla emerges from its impact with a second layer of "balloons" shield unscathed too, gently landing on its tires and park-
ing in place.

Jane is on her feet and pacing determinedly away from her car.

Her shoes echo loudly and forcefully against the metal floor and
blank walls as she strides angrily along a long corridor to an office door.

The chief bureaucrat's disembodied voice resounds in Jane's ears
as she bursts through a closed door into a dimly lit office.

"Are you mad Drake!? What the hell do you think you're doing,
coming here now! Do you know how much it would cost to re-
place that vehicle, and you to boot!?"

Jane replies calmly, "Yes, I know your priorities, but it's nice to
know that you still care about me almost as much as the car."

As her eyes adjust to the low light environment she can finally see
the chief bureaucrat sitting behind his desk, although his features
remain vague.

"This had better be important!" chief bureaucrat says in a still unsympathetic tone.

Jane, remaining calm, says, "Are you done yelling, Chief Crat?"

"Damn you drake!"

Jane smiles sardonically, saying almost to herself, "My turn. Time for you to listen." Then loudly, "So shut up!"

Ever more ferocious thunder is echoing with an intensity that permeates even the subterranean catacombs sheltering Chief Crat's offices.

Although the cavernous office is ostensibly sound-proof, far from the storm on the surface, Jane's flashing eyes make direct hits on a now almost cowering Chief Crat.

Deafening thunderous roars shake Chief Crat as they bellow from Jane's strong lungs and vocal cords.

Jane's harangue is interspersed with words making Chief Crat involuntarily shudder inside: "contemptible" "unacceptable" "corrupt" "inhumane" "bungling" "dictator-ship" "torture" "collapsed legal system" "irresponsible" "human rights" and finally, "I've had enough!"

Agent Jane Drake resigns, turns, and leaves before Chief Crat is able to open his mouth and emit a sound.

In the Tesla again, Jane emerges from the tunnel to see dawn off in the distance, in the central city on the farthest horizon. The storm ends as abruptly as it begins.

Jane soon enters a DTD (Distant Transportation Dock), leaving her Tesla Roadster for robotic repossession by government order.

As this is happening, the wall back in Chief Crat's office displays Agent Jane Drake's file. "UNAUTHORIZED RESIGNATION" blazes across the wall in flashing letters, then:

"EMERGENCY RESIGNATION
PROTOCOL ACTIVATED".

Inside the DTD Jane pushes a button and reads: "ITINERARY CONFIRMED".

A compartment door opens to reveal a space-capsule-like moulded seating unit. Jane enters and sits, pulling both sides of a full space-suit-like garment together.

The sides close and latch. Jane pushes a holographic button labelled "BEGIN VOYAGE". Jane closes her eyes.

While she drifts into REM sleep, the wall in Chief Crat's office displays Jane's DTD file. A notation is added:

"ITINERARY MODIFIED. DRAKE EN ROUTE."

Jane awakens from her first pleasant sleep in years and finds herself inside a holiday cottage like interior.

Photographic illustrations of holiday spot attractions appear on every wall as her eyelids open. Partner is lying beside her, still asleep.

Partner gently awakens saying, "Good Morning, darling." Then stretching and yawning, adds, "That was quite a trip. Ready to get going?"

"Roaring to go." Jane beams with excitement. "Thank goodness we're out of that business!"

"It was a very long, bad dream." Partner nods, "Let's get on with our lives now."

Jane and Partner chat happily while they eat breakfast in the cottage kitchenette. The wall illustrates their morning meal celebration as they eat.

A bite surprised by the wall, Jane casually remarks, "That's a new one. Did you order that?"

"Not me." Partner replies with an equally surprised but casual expression. "We can ask them to turn it off."

"Later. Race you to the pool!" Jane is already on her feet, darting for the door.

Too late Partner replies, "Right. Let's..." Partner's words are lost during an inhale and dash to catch up with Jane.

Jane, followed an instant later by Partner, races out the cottage door. A few long strides later they're stopping abruptly in their tracks.

Their faces drop to puzzled and surprised expressions.

"What the..." Partner blurts out, interrupted by Jane.

"This isn't where we're supposed to be. Damn techno-trips!"

"Let's find out where they put us, Jane." Partner says.

"You can take care of that." Jane says, "I'm going to talk with the DTD manager, to find out when we can get out of here."

•••••

The DTD office is almost deserted when Jane walks in.

At almost the same moment Partner is standing in front of the "Village Holographic Information Kiosk Clerk", VHIKC for short.

"Tell me Seven." VHIKC says.

"It must be the model number." Partner thinks, when he hears the novel but clearly non-human greeting.

"Seven what?" Partner jokes, knowing that he has no real audience.

Getting to the point, the only thing that a holograph can truly understand, Partner says, "I want some information."

Uncharacteristically, VHIKC "Clerk Seven" replies with what at first seems to be a recognition of Partner's humour, "Very funny, Seven. But you have things twisted."

Genuinely surprised, Partner stutters out, "I'm..I'm sorry? Isn't this a place for getting information."

"Of course it is, Seven." VHIKC confirms in a hollow tone, nodding almost mechanically. "We're getting information all the time."

"Seven, oh I see." Partner looks at the chronometer. It shows 07:15.

"You're a tad slow. But it's good to know I've come to the right place. Now, have you got any map files?"

"We are never slow. But certainly, Seven!" VHIKC replies with a robotic smile. "How many?"

"One map will be sufficient, thank you." Partner answers.

"Excellent start. Just a moment please. You'd like to submit a map." VHIKC says with lifeless certainty.

"That's not it. I want you to give me a map." Partner corrects.

A hollow laugh comes from the VHIKC image, "Seven!"

"No one. Just one map." Partner tries to simplify, speaking more slowly and clearly while holding up his pointer finger.

"Please give me one map." Partner says, word by word, as if talking to someone with comprehension problems.

Partner presumes that the VHIKC is defective and needs repairs.

Partner is speculating that there may be a general system problem.

That would also account for DTD's error in sending Jane and Partner here instead of to the destination that they stipulated.

A recording starts playing out of VHIKC's mouth imagery, "Please give me a map." with Partner's image alongside.

"Oh, Bravo! Bravo Seven! Good one. We're rather enjoying this comedy routine. Good going." VHIKC says, replicating a member of a comedy audience having a good time.

"Enough!" Partner says impatiently, tiring of the clearly defective VHIKC. "We are not amused. Now are you going to give me a map or not?"

"You know we can't do that. That's not how it works here. It's not authorized. We retain all files permanently. They're classified, you know." VHIKC replies with a simulated puzzled look.

"But thank you very much for submitting the humour." VHIKC says with a simulated smile. "Of course we'll file it under 'theatre of the absurd' with the very best."

"Are you familiar with the ancient "Who's on first." routine." VHIKC says. "We can play it for you. Just a moment. Here we go."

"Forget it!" Partner quickly takes long strides away, head shaking in dismay.)

"We never forget. It's not possible." VHIKC says as Partner's back disappears along a pathway.

Many steps away, Partner hears the faint recorded voices of the ancient comics Abbott and Costello talking about base-ball.

VHIKC is simulating loud laughter at the comedy routine that it does not actually understand.

Then VHIKC shouts after Partner, "Is there anything else you can do for us today?"

VHIKC is scanning Partner from the back. A red light goes from Partner's head to toe, followed by a supermarket scanner beep tone as the scan is completed.

A display of Partner's photo and DNA pattern reflects in the holographic clerk's vision sensors. The word "Seven" appears under Partner's photo.

"POSITIVE MATCH" appears.

In a normal voice, to itself, VHIKC says, "Seven. Thank you."

Partner notices the red light coming from behind, turns, and shouts: "Why is VHIKC scanning me?"

"Oh, you know, for statistics and insecurity purposes. It's just standard procedure, as usual. We'll be seeing you, Seven!" VHIKC responds.

Partner turns away again and continues walking in more determined steps, retorting in a lower voice, "Not bloody likely. You'll be getting repaired soon enough."

VHIKC's sensors receive Partner's low volume words.

"Seven is sounding just like Costello. Very good. More humour. Another satisfied customer. Already enjoying a happy stay with us." VHIKC records in memory.

VHIKC's vision censors receive a message:

"MISSION ACCOMPLISHED!
WE'LL BE SEEING YOU!"

Meanwhile, Jane has to wait a few minutes in the DTD office before someone wearing an insecurity shirt steps out of an interior door into the still empty entranceway area.

"Nobody is here. Perhaps I'm lost. Could you direct me to the DTD reception, please." Jane says.

"DTD reception? Oh, you must be lost." the insecurity T-shirt wearer says with a smirk.

"Yes, exactly." Jane says, still relaxed from her good sleep.

"Then you'll have to go to "Lost and Found".

"How's that?'' Jane smirks back.

"Just follow the two signs. Someone will tell you what to do there." the insecurity T-shirt wearer walks toward another door, as if in a hurry to go somewhere else.

Calling after the T-shirt wearer, Jane asks an essential question, "Which two signs."

Looking back at Jane, vaguely smiling, "There's only one sign. Look over there. We'll be seeing you!"

Jane sees a sign marked "Two" with an arrow.

She follows subsequent "Two" sign arrows around a twist-ing path and stairway, up a hill to an ornate but small round domed building with a sign on the door. It reads: "LOST AND FOUND".

Jane enters and finds herself inside the rotunda of the dome. At the centre of the floor she can see a huge water lily sitting in the middle of a pond. Its petals are closed.

The petal opens as the doors that Jane has just entered slide closed behind her. Female Holographic Figure (FHF) "TWO" rises and stands inside the petal.

A wall projection begins showing Jane entering the DTD office a few minutes earlier, being greeted, and having her subsequent conversation with the "insecurity" T-shirt wearer.

"Six! Hallo!" Two says.

Not repeating the unfamiliar "Six Hallo!" greeting, Jane begins her service complaint, "FHF, there seems to be some mistake in our itinerary, perhaps a holotypo."

"Oh, Six! Don't be so formal. Please call me Two like everyone else."

"Alright, Two. We have to straighten this out. Partner and I..."

Interrupting Jane, as if correcting her, Two says, "Oh, Seven!

To herself Jane thinks, "Numbers must be expletive place markers in the speech programme here."

Then, addressing Two again, Jane says, "You see, we aren't sup-posed to be here. There's been a mistake."

"Oh dear, Six. Don't worry. This sort of thing happens all the time. Everyone who comes in here says the same thing."

Speaking to herself again, Jane says, "It doesn't surprise me in the least." "General DTD systems failure." Jane is thinking. "The storm must have hit a main component."

Then, addressing Two again, "So you can help us get out of here."

"Now, now. You've only just arrived. Let's not go that far. It's not such a bad place, our little village. We have all the amenities you know."

"Isn't your cottage satisfactory?

"We can re-programme it to meet your specifications, you know."

While Two is saying the last words, the wall begins illustrating alternate interior designs, underscored with the words, "ALL MODELS AVAILABLE".)

"We want you to feel comfortable here, relaxed, and especially talkative." Two says.

Jane responds in a conciliatory tone, "I'm sure it's very nice here, but, as I said, this isn't our itinerary. It's a mistake."

"Just a moment, Six. I'll check our records." Two replies simulating a good hotel-keeper.

Two scans Jane with a red light, followed by a supermarket scanner beep tone as the scan is completed.

Two's eyes become a holographic display of Jane's identification photo and her DNA profile, with "Six" underscoring it. "POSITIVE MATCH" appears next.

Vision censors returning to the appearance of almost normal eyes, Two says, "It's as usual. The system is never wrong, Six. This is you.

"VHIKC has already confirmed Seven too." Two says, in a simulated reassuring tone.

The wall illustration replays the scanning and information dossier of Partner.

"You're in the right place." Two says, simulating confidence.

"We want out of here." Jane retorts.

"Six, I'm sorry. You're in an air tight contract. There are no refunds and no exchanges. There's no way out. This is where you belong." Two says, simulating authority.

"I suppose I'm going to have to go over your hollow head. Who runs this place? I want to talk to the boss, your number one." Jane says.

"Oh, that would be telling. You can't do that. Number One talks to no one, not here, not ever.

"It's a regulation, a policy, a rule, a new insecurity law, if you will.

"Someone in your job should know all about that sort of thing. You know how all the insecurity laws work. That goes doubly for this place." Two says bureaucratically.

"This place?" Jane says, "Where exactly is this place? Where are we?"

"Why, in the village, of course." Two says, almost looking puzzled.

"Who are you?" Jane asks.

"Don't be silly. I'm Two, of course. Your partner is Seven, and you are Six."

"You're the silly ones." Jane laughs, "We have names you know. We're not holographs or itinerary numbers, and you know it."

"Know? No, no." Two says, almost emotionally. "Those aren't itinerary numbers. They're your numbers."

"What do you mean?" Jane says in real life puzzlement.

"It's for statistics and insecurity reasons you know. It's as usual." Two replies as if talking to an ordinary person who will submit to anything that bureaucracy commands.

"What do you want?" says Jane, insisting on an answer she has yet to hear.

"Why, we want information, of course." Two says.

"What do you want to know?" Jane asks.

"Well, to start with, why did you resign?" Two says, readying to make a recording of Jane to determine whether the answer Two expects will be truthful.

"I'm certainly not telling you that. Resigned from what?"

"Six, we must know, for statistics and insecurity reasons."

"Who's insecurity?" Jane demands. "Whose side are you on?"

"Two can play at this game. That would be telling too." Two retorts in a holographic manner.

"I'm surprised at you, Six. Why we're on your side, of course. That's our job.

"We shall always be at your side, behind you, and in front of you, all the time." Two says while appearing to be everywhere around Jane simultaneously.

"Come now, answer the first question so that we can get on to the next." Two says as the wall shows:

"QUESTION ONE: WHY DID YOU RESIGN?"

"I told you I'm not telling!" Jane insists, raising her voice.

"Six, you will. By hook or by crook you will, Six. That's how it works here. We ask. You answer. Just talk to us. There's nothing to worry about."

"We're finished with talking, and I'm not worried at all. Now stop saying Six! Call me by my name, Jane Drake. I'm not a number! I'm a human being. I'm a free person!"

"HA! HA! Good one, Six! VHIKC files told me Seven has a sense of humour too. You are a good couple I see. HA! HA! HA! HA! HA!" Two laughs hollowly.

"Six, listen. You can change. It's easy. Just watch me!"

As Two speaks it changes clothes, body, face, sex, age, race, and voice saying "I'm Two. Me too."

"Which TWO suits you?"

Two resumes the appearance of the original Two greeting Jane when she arrives.

Shaking her head in frustration, Jane turns and walks out. The wall in front of her opens just in time to avoid hitting Jane as she begins to exit.

"We'll be seeing you!" Two shouts toward the disappearing figure.

A holo message appears in front of Jane as she walks away from DTD headquarters:

"THERE'S NO RUSH. WE HAVE PLENTY OF TIME.

YOU CAN TELL US LATER.

PLEASE SLOW DOWN. BE CAREFUL.

WE DON'T WANT YOU TO GET HURT NOW,
DO WE?

YOU'RE MEMORY IS IMPORTANT TO US.

MUSTN'T SPOIL EVERYTHING.

IT'S ANOTHER BEAUTIFUL DAY IN OUR VILLAGE.

ENJOY IT IMMENSELY!

YOU CAN STAY AS LONG AS WE WISH.

WE'LL BE SEEING YOU,
ALL THE TIME
AND
EVERYWHERE!"

Jane and Partner meet at the door of their holiday cottage, noticing the numbers on the outside of the door: Six & Seven.

Stepping inside they're comparing notes.

As they do so, a video illustrates what they say, projecting a recording of each of their encounters onto the cottage wall in front of them.

Jane says apologetically to Partner, "Sorry, I forgot to ask them to turn that thing off.". "So did I." Partner laments.

Using the cottage remote control they each try to shut down the video and search for their present location on a wall projection map.

Now the wall shows Jane and Partner doing just that. "It's very responsive to reality, isn't it?" Jane says. Partner turns up his lips and nods in agreement.

"According to these wall map projections, we don't seem to be anywhere." Jane says.

"It looks like a simulated setting to me." Partner replies. "It might be a holovillage, or a secret overseas prison."

"Maybe, but only the ones running this place are hollow. The in-security person I spoke with appeared to be real." Jane says sceptically.

"I saw other people walking around as well. The village might be real." Jane reports her observations matter-of-factly.

In this very technologically-oriented era, the difference between reality and illusion is becoming increasingly difficult to perceive, even for expert agents like Jane and Partner.

"Hmm. Well then, if the village is real we should be able to find a way out." Partner concludes.

"I didn't see any obvious exits. We'll have to walk as far as we can, find a perimeter, and simply go beyond it." Jane says.

"As you said earlier, we can smell the sea from here. It can't be that far away." Partner reviews what they both know.

We could possibly find a coastline and follow it until we're beyond this place." Partner suggests.

Cautiously glancing at the wall projection recording their every word and action, Jane says, "Let's talk about this somewhere else. The illustration must be broadcasting everything we're doing to a central data log."

•••••

Jane and Partner are far from the cottage, walking briskly along the sands of a very long deserted beach until they reach a curve and find they are not alone.

A small group of people is sitting in chaisses longues under striped umbrellas, playing with beach balls, wading into the water playfully and laughing.

A portly holochef wearing a big apron and floppy chefs hat stands away from a food barbecue and waves enthusiastically at Jane and Partner.

"Six! Seven! Hallo! Hallo! I'm Twenty-Nine, welcome to the Village beach party. You are the latest arrivals and guests of honour!" the holochef says exuberantly.

"Twenty-nine?" Partner says with incredulity. "You don't look a day over 40."

"I was warned about your sense of humour, Seven. Oh it's so good of you both to come! We've been expecting you. " holochef says.

"It was a bit short notice, but everything's under control now. Please join us. Not too tired we hope. What would you like?"

"To get out of here." Jane replies in a tone mocking the holochef's exuberance.

"Now, now, don't be rude, Six. You could hurt our feelings, if we had any. HAA! Seven is updating my humour programme!" holochef says.

"Come now. You can finish your stroll on the beach later. Come on. Even I'm famished, and I never eat.

"You've come a long way today, and without stopping for tea. After all your walking and all that fresh air you've been breathing, you must be starving." holochef says.

"I've lost my appetite for this place, but I could use something to eat." Partner says. "Some energy can help me get away from it all."

"Me too. We've been walking for hours and it looks as if we still have a long way to go for that getaway." Jane says.

"Good-oh! Time for some revitalizing. There's plenty of food and drink for all. You can have anything you want. Eat to your full. We've got all your favourites." the holochef says with a broad smile and the image of a rolling belly.

"How did you manage that?" Partner asks.

"Vital statistics, of course. Meal selection records are standard files, especially "special meal" orders.

"You of all people should know that everything about everyone is kept on permanent file, for insecurity reasons, of course." the holochef says in a pedantic manner.

"Right." Partner says, feeling embarrassment about his former occupation.

"Do you mind if we ask you a few questions?" Jane queries.

"Well done. Spoken like a true professional." the holochef says, almost abandoning his jovial manner.

"But relax. You're not on the job here. Just enjoy yourselves. Leave all the questioning to us." holochef says.

"Remember our Village motto: Questions are a burden on others. Answers make prisoners of us all." the holochef smiles broadly, bordering on unpleasant mischievous.

"Well, we are on this shore to get away from it all." Partner quips.

"Definitely." Jane copies Partner's mannerism. "That's why we're walking here along the beach.

"We're just wondering how much farther we have to walk to cross the perimeter to leave everything here behind."

"Oh! Wonder as you wander no more, Six and Seven. Your destination is just around the next curve in the beach." holochef says, pointing in the opposite direction.

"That lovely cottage in our village is always awaiting your return after each lovely day you spend here.

"We know you've had a big day today. You can soon have a good night's sleep too.

"You'll need it after all the good exercise and scrumptious food you're about to eat.

"Feel free to make a notation in our village oral daily diary file before dozing off." holochef says.

"Feel free." Partner agrees, "That's exactly what we want to do."

"Then, for starters, be sure to mention why you resigned in our Village Daily Diary. That's a very popular story with our subscribers here." holochef says.

"We publish everything that fits and there are no limits. You can have your own column, both of you.

"We'd love to find out everything you have to say about everything. We'll be glad to file anything and everything you can tell us.

"You don't have to hold back, you know. Feel free to blabber." holochef says.

"Oh, give it up! We're not going to be blabbering to any-one." Jane says emphatically.

"Well, if you want a more structured approach, you can fill out our daily survey tomorrow too, and every day. You already know how it starts, with:

QUESTION ONE: WHY DID YOU RESIGN?"

holochef says.

"You're missing the point." Partner says, head shaking in dismay.

"Hm. Private people. We know you both have strong beliefs too. Perhaps you could simply confess to the Village Vicar." holochef says, almost with twinkling eyes.

"If you were really that well-informed about us, you'd know what we actually believe in, freedom." Jane retorts.

"Non-denominational. No matter. You can give a lecture on freedom and resigning at the Village Varsity, based on personal experience, of course." Holochef persists.

•••••

The next day begins with a noisy sleep disruption at dawn.

A disembodied voice that seems to come from everywhere around all at once announces:

"GOOD MORNING! GOOD MORNING, SIX!
GOOD MORNING TO YOU TOO, SEVEN!
RISE AND SHINE!
IT'S ANOTHER LOVELY DAY IN THE VILLAGE! MAKE
THE MOST OF IT! TALK A LOT!

EXERCISE YOUR RIGHT TO FREEDOM OF SPEECH!
SPEAK OUT AND SPEAK UP!
GO AHEAD!
TELL US EVERYTHING YOU KNOW.
YOU CAN MAKE THIS DAY
ESPECIALLY MEMORABLE
FOR US ALL!

FILL OUR FILES WITH YOUR MEMORIES!
GOOD MORNING! GOOD MORNING!"

The wall illustration begins displaying mass rallies of cheering and shouting crowds smiling and waving at "Village Heroes" being honoured for their information giving skills.

"Is it six or seven in the morning? Make up your mind! What do I have to do to get a full night's sleep here?"

"Shush!" a bleary-eyed Jane insists. "Don't say that! They'll think you've cracked."

A micro-instant later an annoying jingle reminiscent of the long gone Internet era of generations ago rings in Jane's and Partner's heads.

Putting pillows over there heads has no effect.

"TELL US RIGHT AWAY,
AND YOU CAN SLEEP ALL DAY!"

"See what I mean!" Jane bristles, no longer groggy or half asleep.

"All right. How about this: What's the best escape route out of here?" Partner jokes.

At the precise moment Partner utters his last syllable another annoying jingle starts.

"TRY TO ESCAPE ALL DAY,
YOU'LL NEVER GET AWAY, HEH!"

"Don't encourage them! Be quiet!" Jane insists.

Partner goes silent, pointing at the door with a thumbs up gesture. Jane nods, saying "Heh! In a musical tone mocking the jingles.

"Oh, my head. They must have put something in the food." Partner almost whispers, grimacing and blinking.

"In your case, it was the drinks. You should know better than to accept unchecked beverages, especially in our present situation." Jane scolds.

"Lucky we're immune to mind rape drugs." Jane adds.

"Sorry. It was irresistible." Partner says more softly.

"You know that's exactly what they're counting on." Jane sighs as she says the words.

"They're counting all right." Partner says, glancing at a holographic newspaper front page headed VILLAGE DAILY DIARY. But it's blank.

Partner inadvertently touches an electronic stylus. Immediately "COLUMN SEVEN" appears on the wall display.

Partner looks at Jane and begins sketching an eye.

"More of your graffiti?" Jane laughs. "I knew you were meant to be a great artist."

Partner smiles and adds arms and a parachute to the eye.

"Clever graffiti. You'll drive them crazy trying to analyze that one. Maybe it will spark some thinking among the other 'guests' too." Jane says.

There's an electronic sound mimicking a knocking at the door.

"Come." Partner says, too late to retract the invitation.

Holographic Recreation Director (HRD) passes through the door, without opening it.

"Good Morning Six, Seven. Are we all ready to go? We have a busy day ahead of us. First a little warm up. Then we'll get into our daily, morning exercises." HRD says.

"We usually go for a run. Just point us in the right direction. We'd be glad to run until we get to the way out."

"That's what we like, good spirits in the morning. Get off to a happy start. But that's not the kind of exercise I'm talking about." HRD says.

"I'm in charge of memory exercises. We don't want you to forget anything before you start talking. Let's start with something simple. Who are you?"

"I'm Jane Drake, and this is...". HRD cuts off Jane in mid sentence, startling her by its reaction to her name.

HRD almost takes on a baffled expression, as it freezes and goes silent.

A wall projection intercedes:

"NON-JURISDICTIONAL RESPONSE PROTOCOL.
ARCHIVES RETRIEVED.

'NAME': ARCHAIC FORM OF ADDRESS;
ABANDONED FOR IMPERFECTION
AND INEXACTITUDE
IN LATE POST-DEMOCRATIC ERA,
150 YEARS BEFORE PRESENT.

CONFUSION ARISING DUE TO
MULTIPLE REPETITIONS
AND DUPLICATIONS
OF IDENTICAL 'COMMON NAMES'.

NAMES SUPPLANTED BY
NUMBER SYSTEM,
MAKING EACH INDIVIDUAL
UNIQUE AND DISTINCT
FOR FILE.

HISTORIC BREAKTHROUGH
IN PERSONAL IDENTIFICATION."

Jane looks directly into the centre of the wall display, saying in a barely audible and puzzled tone, "Why are we only 'six' and 'seven' instead of more complex and lengthy integers."

Wall replies: "IN OUR VILLAGE LIFE IS SIMPLE."

As if hearing a cue to begin speaking again, HRD suddenly reanimates.

It says, "'Jane', what's 'Jane'? Oh, don't be silly, Six. Come now. You must play by the rules here like everywhere else.

"I can make it easier for you to identify yourselves. Let me give you a hint. You're very close, only one apart, between five and eight." HRD says.

"Split shifts?" Partner quips.

"Lovely joke." HRD says without laughing, almost impatiently,

"Of course you know the answer. It's easy. Six and Seven, just like the embroidered symbols on all your clothing."

Jane and Partner look at their shirts. "Six" and "Seven" appear on them as HRD speaks.

"There's a reminder you can always remember. Now let's move along to the main exercises.

"We'll start with a board game. They're very good for the memory you know. Please follow me." HRD says.

"This, I have to see." Jane says, walking after HRD and mocking its pseudo-athletic movements.

Jane, Partner, and HRD emerge from the holiday cottage and find themselves in a large central plaza with a giant outdoor chess board in the middle.

The chess pieces are people wearing identical uniforms embroidered with different numbers.

Each player holds up a banner identifying the game piece that she or he represents. In addition, each player has a sentence illustrated on his or her back.

One player's sentence says, "Quit to switch sides?"

Another player's sentence says, "Secrets for sale?"

Another player's sentence says, "Seduced to treason?"

Yet another says, "Terrorist sympathizer?", etc.

"All right, off we go!" HRD orders play to get underway.

"It's all up to you Seven. You've got the first move. All you have to do is read the sentence on the pawn representing you." HRD says.

"We're not playing!" Jane says emphatically.

"I'm addressing Seven, but... You don't like this game, Six. Oh, such a pity. Never mind. We have plenty of other sports and games to play in our village.

"How about a little memory-jogging?" HRD smiles.

"If you prefer extreme sports, we can offer you some water-boarding, brain-bungee-diving, skinny-dipping-strip-search, sporadic-electric-shocking-stretching, or cavern-exploring-dog-sniffing.

"Really, you name it. We've got it." HRD says.

"I know some of these games may sounds old-fashioned to you, but some people in our village get quite a memory jolt out of them.

"Suddenly they remember everything and become quite lucid. They're more than willing to talk about their life experiences, all their experiences.

"They offer us information lectures." HRD says.

"We don't play games and we don't give lectures." Jane and Part-ner reply simultaneously.

"Oh, come now, Six and Seven. Be good sports, won't you. Besides, Six, it's Seven's move now, not yours. Maybe Seven wants to play."

"Didn't you hear me? Aren't you a team player?" HRD says.

"Yes and No. Of course I heard you and board games aren't team sports." Jane says.

"Then why did you reply when I spoke to Seven?" HRD curls its illusory lips.

"My partner isn't Seven and I'm not Six." Jane says.

"Oh dear! I don't know whether I can help you if you don't want to do any memory exercises. This game may be too late for both of you." HRD says with a simulated pout.

"It's apparent that your memory is already so far gone that you don't even remember your numbers."

"We don't have numbers. We have names. We're human beings." Jane says.

"Oh dear. Oh dear. Oh dear. The orderlies are coming." HRD says, jumping frantically into the air and pointing out Jane and Partner to the approaching holographs in white smocks.

Then HRD seems to be running away. It simply disappears in mid stride. Only HRD's voice is audible, saying, "We'll be seeing you!"

Tiny drones fly toward Jane and Partner. Chess players flee, scattering in all directions. Drones fire on Jane and Partner. Direct hits. Both fall to ground in a daze.

•••••

Jane and Partner awaken from their stunned state inside a building bearing a sign reading: "VILLAGE HOSPITAL".

A doctor is standing over Jane, who is lying in a hospital bed. Partner is in the next bed, unconscious.

A wall illustration begins showing the doctor, Jane, Partner, and their interactions.

"Are you all right, Six." the doctor says.

Almost unconscious, Jane's drugged-like voice manages to say, "I'm not Six." Then she passes out.

•••••

Jane and Partner are now in the doctor's office, lying on matching couches alongside each other. For the first time since arrival, they're tied in restraints.

The doctor is sitting on a nearby arm chair, holding up an electronic stylus as if about to write something in the air.

A wall projection begins showing Jane and Partner being taken from hospital beds, rolled on gurneys, and tied in restraints on couches.

Then the wall projection begins showing the doctor, Jane, and Partner beginning their present conversation.

"I hope you two are feeling better now." the doctor says. "Sorry about the restraints. They're for insecurity reasons."

"Would you like to drink with a straw?" the doctor cordially offers like the host of an afternoon tea party, "Or would you prefer a spot of intravenous tea?"

Struggling to unbind, Partner says, "You must be kidding."

"I can do that. It's in my bedside manner training. But, no, no. We don't kid here. This is a serious institution. We leave the kidding to you." the doctor says.

"I understand that you're the famous Six and Seven and you've come to grace our little Village Theatre with some of your wonderful comedy routines.

"I've brought you here to personally welcome you and to ask for your autographs. We can remove the restraints in a few minutes so that you can sign."

Her hopes rising slightly at the sight of an apparently human professional, Jane says, "There's been a mistake and we don't find it at all funny. We're not here to put on any kind of show. I'm not Six."

"And I'm certainly not Seven." Partner interjects. "We're both adults."

The doctor is noting in the air with electronic stylus, then winking, "Yes, I understand."

"You big stars like your privacy. You're travelling under pseudonyms, incognito so to speak." the doctor winks again.

"No doctor, we're really not Six or Seven." Jane says.

"That's Six and Seven. Hm. I see." the doctor says, scribbling vigorously in the air.

"Mm Hm. Well, we could try some tongue-looseners and talk stimulants.

"Do you have any allergies to truth serums or have you suffered any psychotic episodes following memory probe chip implants?" the doctor poises his pen, ready to note any vital facts.

"Oh, we both definitely do have all those problems." Jane says, mocking the doctor's questions.

We both also have extremely unmovable tongue syndrome. We're quite taciturn by nature too."

With a professionally serious expression, stroking a Freud-like beard, the doctor says, "I see. So we'll have to avoid those kinds of treatments and try something else."

Noting Jane's facetious answer as if it were factual, the doctor says, "But first I'd like to know how long have you... ah... not been Six and Seven?"

"As long as we can remember." Partner says.

The doctor scribbles vigorously in the air again.

Raising two eyebrows at once, the doctor says, "Just as I suspected... massive memory loss." "Don't worry." the doctor smiles reassuringly.

"You've come here just in time. It's not too late. We can fix you up. You'll be back on the stage in no time. I guarantee it.

"Nurse! We have patients requiring emergency memory restoration treatment. We'll be seeing you!" As the doctor speaks, Jane and Partner pass out.

• • • • •

Wall illustrations show Jane and Partner floating separately and apart at different locations in misty air.

Jane is alone, holding her head in an unclear foggy location. A holo replica of Jane's voice is constantly repeating, over and over again, "I am Six. I am Six. I am Six."

Partner too is alone, head in hands in a similarly nebulous location.

A holo replica of Partner's voice is constantly repeating, over and over again, "I am Seven. I am Seven. I am Seven."

•••••

In what seems like only a moment after being restrained in the doctor's office, Jane and Partner are together again, hearing holo replicas of their own voices repeating in unison:

"We're Six and Seven! Welcome to our show! What do you want to know? We can tell you fast or slow! So.... Let's go go go!"

Jane and Partner are standing together on stage inside a building bearing the marquee "Village Theatre Presents: Six and Seven!"

Off stage, the voice of an unseen "master of ceremonies" introduces the entertainment duo:

"AND NOW, (drum roll), FOR OUR VERY OWN ENTER-TAINMENT, OUR VERY OWN VILLAGE THEATRE PROUDLY PRESENTS, FROM THE FAR CORNERS OF OUR VILLAGE, THE FUNNIEST DUO YOU'LL EVER HEAR IN THESE PARTS! (drum roll) THE MASTERS OF INFORMAT-IVE HUMOUR! (drum roll) THE KEEPERS OF LAUGHABLE SECRETS! (drum roll) PLEASE WELCOME, SIX ANNNND SEVEN! (cymbals crash)"

An unseen ragtime band plays a vaudevillian introductory tune. The sound of wild applause and cheers come from an invisible holo audience.

Jane and Partner run on stage, dressed in vaudeville comic costumes, straw hats and red stripped jackets over white pants.

Jane's jacket bears a huge, comic script "Six". Partner's costume bears a similar "Seven".

"Thank you. Thank you." Jane shouts over the din, bowing comically with Partner. I'm Six."

"You don't look half your age." Partner says.

There's a drum roll and a crash of cymbals again and the holo audience laughs wildly and long on cue.

"And I'm Seven." Partner says, "Thanks folks, your laughs are rejuvenating."

More holo audience laughs and cheers follow.

"We're here to tell you stories that will turn your heads and your stomachs!" Jane and Partner say loudly in unison, to more lively applause and laughter.

Again in unison, "We're hear to fill all your files with, you guessed it, innnnnformation!"

Louder, more enthusiastic waves of laughter roll across the air.

"Tell me, Seven, what happened to you on the way to the village?" Jane says like a real comic.

"Did you ask me what happened to me on the way to the village, Six?" Partner asks.

"That's right, Seven." Jane says.

"Why, I resigned, Six." Partner delivers the punchline to more uproarious laughter, then dead silence.

"That's funny, Seven. So did I!" The holo audience applauds, then laughs louder still.

"Why in the world did you do that, Six?" Partner asks.

"I don't remember!" Jane cries out in a clowning tone. The holo audience becomes hysterical.

"That's funny, Six. I don't remember either!" Partner delivers the punch line again, slamming a cane on the stage.

The hysterical laughter becomes deafeningly loud, drowning out the voices of Jane and Partner.

A large hook appears from behind Jane and Partner, pulling them both back and under the curtain. They fall down as they vanish beneath the curtain.

The holo audience starts booing and shouting cat calls, finally shouting, "WE'LL BE SEEING YOU!", then laughing mechanically.

Jane and Partner are lying passed out on the back stage floor.

The holo stage manager (HSM) throws a bucket of water on them, which turns into confetti, awakening them with their own sneezes.

HSM has TWO embroidered on its jacket.

"Good try Six and Seven." HSM says with unconvincing sympathy. "Maybe I can book you in the broom closet next time.

"You're going to have to come up with some new material. The same old lines are getting stale in this town." HSM says.

"You have to put more pizzazz in your act too... you know, more information.

"But how..." Partner says, almost convincingly.

"We're trying our best..." Jane takes on a sorrowful clown facial expression.

"I'll tell you what." HSM says.

"You beef up the information, tell the audience everything you know about everything, and I can almost guarantee you a booking right out of this place.

"You can kiss our Village goodbye and go on to the big time. All we want is information." HSM says with a twinkle.

"You're asking too much, far too much, far too... TWO! That's you!" Jane protests with humour.

"Why sure it's me! Who do you think I am, High Five? Two slaps Jane lightly on the hand. HA-HA-HA-HA-HA!" Two almost simulates a real laugh.

"You're no comedian..." Partner says.

"...and neither are we. Let's get out of here." Jane grabs Partner by the arm and rushes for the back stage exit sign.

They throw off the costume pants, jackets, and shirts, running out of the theatre in only black tights.

Beckoning to the fast disappearing dark figures, Two says, "Ah come on! Can't you Two take a joke? Get it? Two take a joke! HA-HA-HA-HA-HA-HA! We'll be seeing you!"

The dark night sky outside the theatre lights up with Two's pun line.

"Ha..Ha..." Jane repeats unemotionally.

"Ha... We don't get it." Partner adds.

"And neither will you." Jane shouts.

•••••

Overhead this message appears in the brightening sky:

"AIR SURVEILLANCE REPORT:
LOCATION: VILLAGE SQUARE,
HOLIDAY COTTAGE, AND BEACH"

The sky displays multiple images of each location, zeroing in on Jane and Partner opening their eyes in the holiday cottage. It's morning.

They're rising already fully dressed, grabbing backsacs beside the bed, and starting to run out the door and across the square toward the beach.

They don't stop running until they arrive on the sand, pull an abandoned rowboat out to the water, and begin paddling madly away from shore.

They paddle far out of sight of the beach and pass out, exhausted. When they awaken they are out of sight of all land.

"We did it!" Partner shouts happily. "We finally got away from that awful place! That rowing practice paid off."

"I can't believe that they were never suspicious of our sudden interest in oars. We should celebrate, but we didn't bring anything to celebrate with." Jane replies with equal enthusiasm.

"A small oversight. We can always dive for fish and have some sashimi." Partner says.

"Mm. I love Japanese food." Jane opens her eyes wider.

Jane and Partner are soon diving off the boat and swimming playfully with fish. Later, back on board, they're devouring sashimi from their catch.

"Delicious!" Jane says, "You can do wonders with such a small knife. We should do this more often."

"I think we'll be getting tired of this menu before we finally land somewhere." Partner says.

"I've seen some birds over that way.", Jane says, pointing at a horizon in the opposite direction from which they have paddled.

"All right. Let's head that way. Someone there should be able to tell us where we are, and then we can finally go wherever we want to go." Partner says.

"I'm for that." Jane smiles broadly. "We'll avoid DTD this time."

•••••

As Jane and Partner draw closer to land, they anchor their small row boat and swim to shore, arriving at a forested area along a secluded, empty beach.

Three hundred metres away, people in desert Arab clothing are walking along the beach toward the trees.

As they get closer to the landing site of Jane and Partner, their voices become audible. They're speaking Arabic.

Jane steps out from behind the trees, gradually revealing her presence, and greets them in their language. She asks directions to the nearest settlement.

They point along the shoreline and inland. Jane thanks them. They resume their walk, heading farther along the sands.

When they are almost out of sight, Jane turns toward the woods and waves out Partner.

"You can come out of the woods now. We'll be fine. We have to head this way." Jane says, leading Partner to their destination.

On the edge of the settlement Partner says, "I'll practice my Arabic this time."

"Go to it." Jane says encouragingly.

Partner approaches a passerby and asks in Arabic which way to go for overnight accommodation.

"C'est dans cette direction, Monsieur." the passerby says, pointing toward some bleached white walls. "Merci beaucoup, Monsieur." Partner replies.

"It's a good thing you speak French too." Jane smiles teasingly at Partner.

"It's definitely, North Africa." Partner says.

"Good. I love Africa. We can try the local figs, nuts, and halawa or halva, then head south for couscous." Jane says.

"Sounds scrumptious. Follow me." Partner says.

They walk into the settlement. It appears to be a relatively small village.

Jane and Partner don't notice the air surveillance showing them walking into a central market filled with vendors selling many types of irresistible food and other items.

"What a sight for sore eyes." Jane beams, ready to eat.

"Welcome back to the free world." Partner beams back.

They stroll around the market sampling, bargaining, and buying food, picking up odds and ends for souvenirs.

"This is wonderful!" Jane's face is flush with happiness.

"After all we've been through lately, we deserve this break. Let's stay for a while." Partner says as Jane literally jumps for joy.

"I think I saw a small inn over there. Let's see if I'm right." Jane says.

Hand in hand, Jane and Partner smile warmly at their new surroundings and walk slowly, enjoying every sight on the way to a small inn and while choosing a small cottage.

As they enter, the wall hangings change designs and colours. The decor is traditional Arab.

Admiring the hangings, Partner says, "That's a nice touch."

"Hm. I like these Arabian futons." Jane says. "They're much more comfortable than the hard wooden benches in a rowboat.

"I'm so tired." Partner says, almost asleep as soon as he drops onto a futon.

For ten days Jane and Partner savour and celebrate every new flavour and experience of their North African holiday experience.

On the eleventh day they're finally throwing on their backsacs, preparing to paddle away for other parts. Just as they're set to go, there's a knock at the door.

"Come." Partner welcomes the unexpected visitor.

An Arab with a beard, dressed in thobe and ghutra walks in, face in slight shadow, not completely clear.

"Do you speak English?" he asks Jane and Partner.

"We do." Jane replies.

"Lovely." the Arab says, "Mind if I practice with you. English-speakers are so rare nowadays."

"Yes, it's almost a dead language. How did you manage to learn it?" Partner says.

"I studied dead languages at university. I'm with the government here now, visitor relations."

"The owner of this lodge says you're planning to leave us today." the Arab says. "Such a shame.

"Aren't you happy here with us? Have we not shown you enough good hospitality?

"Do our manners and customs offend you? Was someone rude to you? Were you mistreated or cheated?"

"It's wonderful here." Jane reassures their official host. "We have absolutely nothing to complain about.

"The people we've met have been so kind to us. There's nothing at all wrong with this place. Quite the contrary." Jane says.

"Excellent. So you will extend your stay, won't you?" the Arab says.

"I suppose we could, but we really should be heading elsewhere." Partner says very politely, so as not to offend the hospitable stranger.

"Yes, we must go." Jane adds. "It's a small world, but we have a lot of territory to cover."

"Oh, really! I'm so sorry to hear that." the Arab looks down.

"You're quite a sensation here. This is such a small place. People are always talking, you know, about other people's affairs.

"I understand that you came here in a row boat. What great adventure! We don't often get visitors like you." the Arab says.

"So, well, I was wondering." the Arab is suddenly shy.

"Would you be willing to participate in a short visitors' survey before leaving us? It's all very straightforward you know.

"We just want to know all the who, what, when, where, why, and how. It's simply information for statistics, and of course, security purposes."

"I'm not sure we could." Partner replies, trying to remain polite while becoming evasive as his mind replays the recent unpleasant use of the very words the Arab is now saying.

"We're... a... big city people. We're sensitive about answering questions from people we don't know." Partner explains.

"I see. Hmm." the Arab shyly hesitates to impose, then excitedly adds, "Well, ah yes! I know just the trick. Here it is."

Picking up a stylus and waving it in the air, the Arab continues, "You can just read the questions and jot down your answers.

"Or, look over here." pointing at a wall painting which transforms into an illustration screen as he speaks.

"You can just talk to us. You know, I'd really love to invite you to give a talk on your stay here. It would be so nice!

"You can speak about your other travel experiences too and everything else about your lives.

"Please, please, won't you please tell us your story?" The Arab suddenly begins speaking in an almost childlike manner, catching Jane and Partner by surprise.

"You seem to have a lot of technology for such a small place." Jane says, almost suspiciously asking the question that doesn't seem to matter up to now, "Where exactly are we?"

"Whose in charge here, you now, your number one? And, what exactly do you want from us?" Jane says.

"That would be telling." the Arab says, changing from a deep to a higher pitched voice. Jane knows it's a familiar voice.

"Well, let's get on with it." the Arab says. "Here's the first survey question: Why did you resign, Six and Seven?"

"Who are you?" Partner says, already knowing the answer.

"You don't recognize me? Why I'm TWO, of course. Didn't Six tell you I can change? Just watch me."

Two changes clothing, body, face, sex, age, race, and voice saying, "I'm Two. Me too."

Between changes, Two returns to her familiar Two image from our Village. "Which TWO pleases you?" Two says.

"None. Enough of you! Aren't you out of your jurisdiction here?" Jane says.

"Perhaps. Wait and see. We'll be seeing you!" Two says, walking through the door without opening it.

"She never gives up, does she?" Partner says.

"Neither do we. Let's get out of here, now!" Jane says.

A police siren is waling outside. Wall illustration shows a police vehicle pulling up to the Arabian cottage where Jane and Partner are staying.

Two police officers get out of vehicle. There's a loud knock on the door.

"Open up. It's the police." Officer Eh says.

Jane goes to the door, opens it. Two officers display their electro-badges.

"I'm Detective Eh and this is Detective Beh." Eh says.

"I see. Good morning, officers." Jane says. "How can I help you?"

Detective Beh's electro-badge changes to display an image of Jane.

"Your photo just came across the screens in connection with a missing persons case. Would you mind answering a few questions?"

"All right. Who's missing?" Jane says.

"Sorry. We've come to ask you some questions, not the other way around." Beh says, almost apologetically.

"According to the screens, you've been missing for the past ten days. Can you tell us where you've been?"

"Right here." Jane says.

"Have you been alone?" Eh says.

Gesturing toward Partner, Jane says, "No. Look over there."

Looking at Partner, Eh says, "Is that right?"

"Sure, I can vouch for her." Partner says, smiling.

Partner's image appears on Detective Beh's badge screen.

"Oh-oh. Your photo just came across the screens too, in connection with the same case." Beh looks concerned.

"Very well. What's this all about?" Partner says.

"Sorry, as Detective Beh just explained, we've come to ask you some questions, not the other way around." Eh says.

"Hm." Partner sighs.

"We're going to have to take you both downtown for questioning." Detective Eh says.

"How long is this going to take?" Jane says.

"Sorry." Detective Eh says, "As I just...

"I know." Jane interrupts, "You're the ones asking questions here, not us. We'd be glad to try to help you with the missing persons case. Let's go, then."

•••••

At the police department a wall projection shows the two detectives with Jane and Partner, sitting around a table.

"Can we get you something to drink?" Detective Beh says.

Jane and Partner answer simultaneously, "No, thank you." Jane says, "We'd like to keep this short."

"We have the results of your scanning at the entrance door here." Detective Beh says. "They tell us you're the ones we're looking for, all right."

"Fine. Case closed, right? We can go now." Jane says.

"But, we're wondering what this is all about." Partner says.

"Okay, I'll give it to you straight. We're on to you." Detective Beh says.

"I have no idea what you're talking about. On to what?" Jane says.
Detective Eh stands and leans menacingly toward Jane, saying, "So you won't talk, eh? That's okay. We already know everything about you."

Jane, holding back laughter at Eh's old movie line, says, "Good. Then we can go now, right."

As Jane rises to leave, Beh blocks her chair, causing Jane to involuntarily lose her balance for a moment and abruptly sit down again.

"The rough stuff doesn't impress me." Jane says, "So you may as well forget it. We have rights, you know. You can't just detain us without good reason."

"Huh! Where have you been?" Beh retorts, "We got rid of reason a long time ago. That went out with the age of polite airport insecurity.

"The only rights you're going to get from us are these," Beh holds up his right fist but doesn't swing it. "and lefts too if you want."

Detective Eh stands and pulls Detective Beh aside.

"Now, now. This isn't Abu Ghuraib Prison, you know. Let's cool down a little. Ice tea anyone?"

There's a moment of silence while tea is served and the room goes calm.

"Okay. It's like this..." Detective Eh says in a conciliatory tone, "According to the screens and your scans, you're the missing persons and, according to the register at the hotel, you're travelling under assumed names."

"Did you know that travelling under an assumed name is illegal here?" Detective Beh says in a subdued tone, sipping his tea.

The wall alongside the table shows an electronic poster saying: MISSING, with photos of Jane and Partner, along with the words "WANTED FOR QUESTIONING".

"We're obviously not missing. We're right here." Partner says. "And, as for our names, we're not assuming anything. Those really are our names in the hotel register."

Jane adds, with a tone like Detective Eh, "As I said before, case solved and closed."

Then, rising to leave, Jane says, "It's been...(trying to come up with an appropriate word she settles for) an experience meeting you, detectives."

Partner rises too. Detective Eh blocks the door, slowly holding up his hand with a pleading expression on his face, "Please don't rush off. We'd like to make up for the fuss."

"You sure we can't get you another cup of tea? How about some couscous? We can order some and have it delivered right here." Detective Eh says.

"We can have a little chat, you know, talk about life and things, especially your lives." Beh says with a sympathetic grin, "I've never met anyone like you two before.

"What brings you here? Where are you going next? Are you on holidays? When do you have to go back to work? Sorry to be so inquisitive. It's an occupational hazard.

"Or did you quit your jobs? "Why would you do a thing like that, get an offer from the competition? Why else would anyone resign?"

Detective Beh never hesitates to listen to an answer. Jane and Partner smile and shake their heads, motion to leave.

"Goodbye detectives." Jane says, waving with her right palm.

Partner adds, "I believe this interview is finished, isn't it. Thanks for the offer to eat, but we have to be on our way. We can't stomach any more of your official hospitality."

"Sorry, we're going to have to take you into protective custody for obstruction of justice." Detective Eh says.

"What! That's ridiculous. We're not in any danger, and your the ones obstructing here. You're obstructing our freedom and departure. We're leaving, right now." Jane bristles.

Detective Beh pulls out a micro stun gun, saying, "Six and Seven, you're under arrest for assuming names and attempting to escape. Don't make me use this..."

"Wouldn't think of it." Jane says, using Beh's outstretching arm to throw him on top of a very surprised Eh. Both detectives crumple to the floor, stunned by the impact.

"Shall we go?" Partner says.

"Right." a smiling Jane says, "That felt good."

The police wall projection now shows an alarm ringing and calling all available officers to the interview room:

"OFFICERS NEEDING ASSISTANCE!"

"Too late!" Jane says as she and Partner exit the police building. Two micro stun gun beams later, Jane and Partner fall to the ground, conscious but not moving.

Arriving officers pick them up and carry them to a holding cell. A few moments later they are in restraints, being marched back to the interview room.

There is no sign of Eh or Beh. Jane and Partner are alone with someone not wearing a badge. Instead, she has an electro-tag saying, LAWYER.

She says, "Please sit down, Six and Seven. I'm 22. I've been appointed to take your case.

"I should tell you from the outset that the charges against you are very serious and you could face quite a long stretch of imprisonment.

"However, I also have some good news for you too. The police are willing to make a deal." the lawyer says, looking hopefully at Jane and Partner.

"You saw the wall video, right?" Jane says, "So you know the fight with the detectives was self-defence. They threatened us with a stun gun."

"Oh, no. That's not their case. The detectives actually enjoyed the fight you put up. They're reporting it as a training exercise." the lawyer says reassuringly.

"But actually, we're the ones who should be pressing charges." Partner says. "We're the ones being threatened with assault with a stun gun."

"We were merely leaving police headquarters." Jane adds. "I know, they're trying to charge us with "attempting to escape".

"Wrong again." the lawyer looks almost genuinely surprised.

"There's no question of evading legal custody here. That would imply you were being held legally, which of course you were not.

"Furthermore, if it really were against the law to attempt to escape, everyone in our village would be in jail."

"Well, the village is a jail, isn't it?" Jane says.

Agitated by Jane's words, the lawyer raises her voice, "Now see here! This is part of your problem. You're not supposed to be asking questions.

"You must realize that you're not the lawyers and only lawyers can ask questions.

"Witnesses can only answer questions, not ask them."

"Witnesses can only provide the answers to the questions that lawyers ask." the lawyer bristles with professional confidence.

"Ergo, since you two are the key witnesses in your case, your role here is only to listen to my questions and to answer them completely and honestly.

"You have to be truthful and tell us everything, or you won't get out of here, ever."

"Then," Partner begins, thinking out loud, "How can I put it? Ooops! Strike that question from the record. Forget the way I phrased that sentence.

"I'll try to say it another way." Partner chooses his words very carefully in this no-questions-asked setting.

"I was wondering about the 'very serious' charges you mentioned and hoping that you would tell us what they are."

"That's the way to say it!" the lawyer beams, completely ignoring the meaning of the Partner's indirect request.

"Now listen carefully. Here's the deal you're being offered. It's quite simple really." the lawyer says, with all the sincerity of a sleazy corporate mouthpiece facing disbarment.

"All you need to do is cooperate with the authorities. That's us. Just answer a few questions from us and all charges will be dropped. You'll be free to go."

"This is beginning to sound familiar." Jane says to Partner, who nods. "It's the same old tune, all the time. Someone should change the music." Jane says.

"Oh, come now. It's not that bad." the lawyer says as if talking to small children. "If you don't like answering questions orally, you can always submit written confessions."

"That's the whole point! We don't submit to anyone!" Jane shouts back.

The room wall displays a written transcript of the lawyer's words as she says her next lines.

"You don't submit to any One? How about any Two? How many times do we have to tell you that you can just give us your information orally, without questioning?

"Just talk about yourselves. Tell us everything. We'll do all the rest, automatically." the lawyer says.

"We can order your release just as soon as you tell us the whole story about, you know, your resignations, future plans, etc.

"You must understand that we need your details for statistics and insecurity purposes. It's a simple, reasonable, and uncomplicated request." the lawyer concludes as if giving a final summation that a jury is sure to accept.

"You make it sound so easy." Jane says.

"I think I can speak for the both of us." Partner nods as Jane turns away from the lawyer and says, "I hope that will be all right with you."

"Oh, by all means." the lawyer says, as if speaking on behalf of Partner, who frowns at her.

"Do go ahead." the lawyer says. "I know you're a great story teller. I'm looking forward to hearing this one." The lawyer smiles broadly.

The interview wall display zooms in on Jane's mouth.

"Very well. Let's get comfy now. This is going to take a while." Jane says in a tone usually reserved for children.

"Please take your time. No rush." the lawyer says with almost naive hope in her eyes. "We wouldn't want to leave anything out now, would we?"

"Once upon a time there was a pretty little village on the coast of a great sea." Jane begins.

"Quite charming really, at first sight." Partner adds, for colour.

The interview room wall starts showing idyllic images of the village to accompany Jane's words. Faint fairy tale music plays in the background.

"That's where we started this life." Jane says.

The interview room wall shows two small children walking hand in hand, one with an embroidered Six on clothing, the other with a Seven.

"We thought we were in an earthly paradise where every-thing was almost perfect. But it wasn't. One day, on the hillside, we found a big house with a monster inside."

"The monster had very big eyes and very big ears. The eyes and ears were so big that they covered its entire body."

The wall illustration displays eyes and ears so big that they render the monster's face almost invisible.

"Oh my goodness!" the lawyer screams at this sight, like an excited child.

"So the monster could see and hear everything in the village, and the entire world." Jane says, swaying her hands in the shape of a large globe.

"But the monster didn't look at anything or anyone, and it didn't listen to anything or anyone either.

"So the monster actually knew nothing about the world. And, the monster knew nothing about what was going on in the world either."

"The monster also had a mouth. Unfortunately, that too was a problem. The mouth was getting bigger and bigger.

"It was always talking louder and louder. And it was always talking to itself." Jane says, as the wall illustration adds a huge mouth that obliterates the monster's face altogether.

"The mouth was always talking about the world that the monster never actually looked at or listened to.

"Things were getting worse and worse." Jane says.

The lawyers eyes are opening wider and wider as her face becomes flush with wonder while Jane continues the story.

"The monster was always asking questions while it was never looking and listening. So the monster's questions were not very good.

"They were based on the monster's ignorance of the world. The monster's questions sounded very silly." Jane says mockingly.

"And in the end, the monster was only listening to itself and answering its own silly questions. It would have been funny if this creature didn't happen to be a monster."

"As time passed, the monster was gradually talking itself into changing the world, to make it more to the monster's liking." Jane says.

"Oh dear! What happened next?" the lawyer makes a grab for Jane's arm, but Jane pulls it back just in time.

"Partner and I tried to get away from the monster, but it kept catching us and bringing us back."

"What ever could you do?" the lawyer says with a look of dismay.

"There was only one thing we could do." Jane nods at Partner as she completes the phrase.

Almost breathless, the lawyer says, "What was that?"

"We slayed the monster!" Jane shouts. The lawyer is so surprised by this turn in the story that she almost jumps out of her seat.

Partner takes out a mini stun gun concealed in a jacket pocket since it fell out of Detective Beh's hand when Jane threw him.

Partner zaps the lawyer. Her face turns into Two's, then transforms into many other shapes, sizes, and images before finally going blank and vaporizing.

The police wall illustration goes blank and the wall itself disappears.

For a moment, the village is all around Jane and Partner. Just as suddenly, it starts to go out of focus, wobble, and become transparent.

A natural, uninhabited, rural setting, filled with trees and flowers replaces the Village.

"Just as I suspected." Jane says.

"Good story, Jane." Partner says.

"Thanks, but what's that?" Jane points off in the distance.

It's a cottage. They walk toward it and find a door knocker on the outside with only the word "One" engraved on it. Jane knocks.

A voice responds from the other side of the cottage, "Hallo! I'm here in the garden. Do come here for some tea."

Jane and Partner walk around the cottage, in the direction of voice. They find an older woman sitting at a patio table under an umbrella, pouring tea.

"How lovely of you to drop by for tea with me. Now tell me, how are you enjoying your holidays? Please tell me everything." the older woman says.

"This is no holiday." Jane replies.

"Oh, I'm just teasing. I know you two will never tell anyone anything." the older woman smiles warmly.

"I'm glad someone finally understands us." Partner says, relieved.

Assuming a slightly scolding tone, the older woman says, "However, I am a little upset with you two. You're so destructive. Do you realize how much it cost to build the our village hololand?"

"It was a waste of money from the start!" Jane retorts.

Changing demeanour again and sighing, the older woman concedes, "You have made that point eminently obvious.

"I suppose you expect us to hire you back as consultants now, at double your old salaries. You have proven to us that you will never talk.

"Don't worry. Your rehiring is in the budget already. So, please, you must help us to rebuilt. We all want a better world now, don't we?"

"I think we're already well on the way to accomplishing that work. Just look around you. We've done our part." Jane says hopefully. "Now please do yours."

"This is a much better world than your village." Jane says, taking a deep breath of the fresh, clean air.

Agent Jane Drake (retired) is standing in the middle of lush greenery and natural habitat all around some One's cottage and well beyond it, with only seaside on the near edge.

On the opposite horizon rolling hills rise with glacier top-ped mountains behind them.

VOLUMES FROM MYTHBREAKER

Terrian Journals series:
A Sketch of Terrian History
Terrian Journals' How To Make The Nation
500 Years In Louis Bourbon's Few Hectares
Full Employment: Not Fulfilling
Terrian
Terrian Journals: Living as a Newcomer
Middle Earth Journals
Rediscovery Journals
Fukurokuju No Kasumi Journals
Sabbatical Journals
Departure Journals
Adventuredate Unknown Journals
Away Team Journals
Searching For South Journals
Inonakanokawazu Journals
КАЗАНЬ Journals
Exile Journals
Tenjin Journals
Terrian Journals for the Misguided
Terrian Journals' N.S.R.: Not Spying, …Really!
TJ JNG: Terrian Journals' Jokes Nobody Gets
Terrian Journals' Half Serious
Terrian Journals' Disbelief
Terrian Journals' House Trap
Terrian Journals' Virtually Camping
Terrian Journals' Crystal
Virtually Dead
Terrian Journals' Maximum Insecurity
Terrian Journals' Mandarinas
Terrian Journals' Living With Lords
Terrian Journals First Anthology
Terrian Journals Second Anthology
Pre-Terrian Journals:
Explorations Of Inner & Outer Space
Out of Context
Terrian Journals Origins
Archway series:
Archway: Six Year Book of Dreams
Archway: Lifetime Rhyme
Archway's Valentine Love
Archway's Garden Rhymes
Archway's Christmas New Years Rhymes
Additional Titles:
Language Learning Secrets
Trying To Teach Languages In The L.B.E. World
An Adult Book About Education
Terrian Journals' Miss Schooling?

Fiction: Terrian Journals' Political Science Fiction

www.ingramcontent.com/pod-product-compliance
Lightning Source LLC
Chambersburg PA
CBHW060435180626
46817CB00007B/2820